I0789478

8

Emrick

I OPENED THE mists and stepped from the afterlife into Adrian's back garden.

At this time of year, it was nothing short of a winter paradise. Someone had shovelled a network of paths through the snow, creating stops at the ice sculptures of dragons and wolves and a dancing couple. A bench moulded out of snow and protected from the wind by a half-igloo graced the end of one of the paths, and I found Adrian sitting there staring up at the sky. Above us, the clouds had cleared and the stars sparkled through the trees.

"Emrick," he said without looking at me. "Why did I suspect I'd see you tonight?"

I smiled as I approached and settled on the bench beside him. I stretched my legs out in front of me and followed his gaze to the stars. "Because you know me better than I know myself most days. You have for as long as I've known you."

Adrian pressed his lips together in a subtle smirk. "Only because you're not nearly as mysterious as you strive to be, my friend. You transport yourself through the mists, shroud yourself in death and darkness, but at your heart, you're still a person craving connection. As we all are."

I huffed but didn't give him the satisfaction of a verbal response. "She came to you?"

He inclined his head. "She did. I sent her to Toronto with James."

I stilled. "Are you sure that's wise? For either of them?"

My concern earned me a rare full-toothed grin, and his eyes glittered with amusement. "I think it will be good for them. I'm not saying it won't come to blows, but I have faith they'll be able to hold back from outright murdering each other."

I wasn't so sure.

Adrian slid me a look. "She thinks it's Mikhail."

The state of the bodies I'd found, cut up and discarded, flashed through my mind.

"It fits. Their souls told me nothing, but I remember the number of corpses he left behind last time. And the time before that. If she's right, the three we found are nothing compared to what's coming." I pursed my lips and tilted my head back, pointedly not looking at Adrian. "She mentioned passing it off to the witch hunters. Think she will?"

"You know her as well as I do. What do you think?"

"I think she'd rather be tied to the stake again than cede control to a group like that."

"I concur. Which is the primary reason I sent James with her. Since you two refuse to sort out your problems"—he paused, silently emphasizing his opinion on that point—"I thought it best she have support. Her magic is…"

I winced. "I know."

When I'd found Katerina in the remains of Palonia, covered in gore and surrounded by her fallen kin, her magic had been stagnant. Present but leashed. Choked by the pressure she'd put on herself.

It had taken us a hundred years to break down those mental barriers and launch her into the greatness she was destined to achieve.

Before she'd ordered me away, I'd watched the force of her power wane, buried under layers of depression, fear, and self-doubt. Time had worn her down, and I didn't know if the endless flow of years, Adrian's retirement, or the issues between us lay at the root of it.

My heart ached that it was so, but we weren't in a place where she would allow me to help her. Not again. No, if my sorceress wanted to return to the heights she'd once claimed, this time she would need to figure it out for herself.

I prayed to Death she did before Mikhail realized she was hunting him.

"You'll help her?" I asked.

Adrian sighed and leaned against the back of the bench. "I'm tired, Emrick. After two thousand years, I barely have the motivation to source my own meals."

That was the second time I'd heard those words this week, and it worried me. Just how far would their fatigue push them? Kat and Adrian were the only two people anchoring me to my humanity. Their deaths would be challenging to achieve, but if they truly wanted to, they could leave this world. Leave me. And I would be stuck here alone.

My soul shivered in horror, but Adrian left me no time to dwell. "Of course I'll do what I can, but she's as safe under James's protection as she would be under mine." He sniffed a laugh. "Not that she would accept either."

I agreed with him, but that didn't quell the unease swimming in my gut.

Adrian smoothed a crease on his pant leg. "Katerina will be fine. You need to learn to trust that she can take care of herself. Once you do, the two of you will find your way."

I gritted my teeth and again said nothing. He was right, of course, but his advice wasn't easily swallowed. I'd sacrificed fragments of my soul for

Kat over the past nine hundred years, and I would sacrifice a thousand more if it kept her safe. Even at the risk of losing myself.

I refused to regret what I'd done.

She refused to accept what I'd do.

Until one of us gave in, I didn't know how Adrian's prediction would ever come to pass.

9

Katerina

BARRETT AND I reached Toronto on the cusp of ten o'clock.

Even in February the city was awake at this hour, people leaving the theatre, heading to or leaving clubs, restaurants, pubs.

The hum of life, the pace of mortality, rushed through me like a drug, prickling my skin and making my blood dance.

Without fail, the city made me feel alive in ways the isolation of the country never did. Unfortunately, it was a burst of energy that always crashed too soon and left me feeling old and withered. It was why I hated coming here but why I knew I would never stay away forever.

The drive had been tense and uncomfortable, the opposite of my longer drive from Manitoulin to Muskoka.

But of course it was. On my way to Adrian's, I had my favourite music blaring through the speakers and the temperature at perfect Katerina levels. On my way to Toronto, I had Barrett.

It wasn't that I'd hoped the moment we accepted Adrian's decree Barrett's hardened exo-skeleton would melt into human form or anything, but at the very least I'd hoped he would open his mouth and allow sound to pass through his lips.

To be fair, he had, but only to inform me he would drive first to Etobicoke to introduce me to his contact in the witch hunters so I could decide what I wanted to do.

Then he'd clutched the steering wheel in the approved position, stared straight out the window, and focused solely on the road for the next few hours.

I'd hijacked the car's audio, cranked the most obnoxious songs from my favourite playlist—edging the decibels slightly louder than I normally would have just to watch the subtle tic in the corner of his eye—and sat back to watch the scenery fly past us.

Now that we'd arrived, I wondered if he'd talk to me or if we'd have to learn how to communicate through glares and eye rolls. Although I was down for the challenge, I couldn't help but worry it would delay us past the point of function. Mikhail wasn't about to wait for us to understand each other.

To my relief, as he pulled to a stop in the driveway of a comfortable bungalow, Barrett said, "This is where Tony lives. I gave him the heads up we were coming, but don't be surprised if he's not thrilled you're here."

By Barrett's tone, I gathered Tony wasn't the only one.

"Excellent," I said. "I'll fill him in on what I found, hear him out about how he would handle it, and if I like his plan, I'll leave it to him."

I had a sneaking suspicion I wouldn't like his plan.

Part of me wondered why I was wasting time talking to this guy when I could be chatting with the witches at Rune The Day, but I shushed that voice. I wasn't wasting time. I was keeping my options open.

Barrett got out of the car and headed to the front door, leaving me to catch up to him.

The curtains in the picture window fluttered, and a few moments later, the front door opened.

The witch hunter was not what I had expected. Typically, hunters looked like Barrett. Brawny, fit, often with a similar deep scowl. Witch hunter training was rigorous, as they needed to be prepared for anything the dark witches might throw at them, magically or otherwise.

This dumpy little potato looked as threatening as an over-saturated French fry. His glasses were thick, his eyes small, and his graphic tee was stained with what I could only guess was cheese powder. He stood only a few inches taller than me, maybe five-eight, and, if I had to guess, was about twenty-six years old.

"Barrett, it's good to see you." The two of them proceeded to engage in an elaborate handshake.

"Thanks for agreeing to talk to us. I know it's late."

Tony scowled, the expression not nearly as intimidating as Barrett's as it made his already small eyes squinty. "Your text said there's a dark witch causing trouble, so of course my door is open. I wish these fuckers would cast their death magic on themselves and save us the trouble."

He spared me a glance, and I got the impression his wish included more than just dark witches.

Given the witch hunters' tendency to look down on all magic, I was surprised Barrett only had contacts within the organization and wasn't a member himself.

I wondered if his relationship with Adrian disqualified him.

Tony scanned me over with a disdain that might have made me laugh if I hadn't controlled myself. I needed to remember we might want his help.

"You must be the sorceress," he said.

"The one and only." I offered the same smile I gave Barrett when I wanted to ruin his day.

Tony replied with a low hmph, then shifted back to Barrett, making it clear I was no longer welcome in this conversation.

I wasn't bothered that he hadn't asked for my name. Calling me "the sorceress" revealed he knew exactly who I was, and I was impressed he had the confidence to dismiss me. Most witch hunters I met at least made a show of deference, acknowledging that we were on the same team and that I had the power to light their asses on fire if they pissed me off.

"Tell me about this witch," he said to Barrett.

Barrett glanced my way, and I shrugged, happy enough to let him do the talking if it meant getting Tony's view on things.

"Three witches have already been killed somewhere in downtown Toronto. Blood drained. Looks to have been part of some ritual."

"Good riddance," Tony said, and I clenched my teeth.

"We have reason to think Mikhail is behind it, and these dead witches were either a test run or a first step towards something worse."

I watched for any flicker of fear or shock to cross Tony's expression, but it never came. Anger bubbled inside me. "You already know he's in town."

I hated being left out of the loop.

He crossed his arms and shifted his weight on his feet. "We've heard rumours, but our orders are not to engage until we have reason to. If he's not causing trouble in our city outside the covens, we don't want to draw him out. That's how good people die."

Good hunters, he meant. The witches obviously didn't matter.

My anger grew hotter as it radiated up my spine and over my cheeks, tightening the muscles in my jaw. I had to stay calm. We were here for a reason, and it wouldn't benefit me to commit arson.

I repeated the mantra until my blood pressure settled.

"Obviously the situation has changed," he said, as if sensing my difficulty in not slamming his head into the wall for his short-sightedness. "Bodies mean he's not planning to leave, so I'll touch base with the organization and deal with it. Thanks for letting us know."

"On the contrary," I said, stepping forward. My mouth was working independently of my brain, my rationality blocked by the haze of fury, but I couldn't stop myself. "I came here to assure you I had the situation in hand and for the witch hunters to follow my lead."

There it was.

Now that the words were out, I had no choice but to double down. My funk could take a back seat, and my power would have to wake up, because I'd put my foot in it. But I couldn't stand by and let the hunters take over. They could have stopped Mikhail the moment he'd stepped into the city—prevented those witches from dying—and they'd chosen not to because they *didn't want to draw him out*. That wasn't the sort of mentality that would get the job done. My magic was weak, sure, but at least I was willing to do whatever needed to be done.

"Mikhail and I go way back," I said. "It wouldn't feel right letting anyone else have the satisfaction of putting the rabid beast down."

Tony's lip pulled back in a sneer. "I don't think so, sorceress. You may think you're all powerful, but our organization has resources you can't imagine. We can resolve this a lot faster and more cleanly than you can."

History did not support his claim.

I imagined taking another step towards him, revelled in the vision of him stepping back and trapping himself against the wall. I longed to exert my magic and put him in his place. He thought the hunters were the better option, but they took a wide-net approach, while I preferred a targeted attack. They wouldn't care who they killed around Mikhail as long as they got him. Mundanes were liable to stand witness to the carnage, and they or their memories would need to be cleaned up.

I'd been here a thousand times before. His boasts were laughable.

But I couldn't afford to alienate him more than I already had. The truth remained that Mikhail was powerful, my magic was weak, and the hunters did, in fact, have resources I lacked.

"A joint venture, then," I suggested. "I save your organization the legwork, and you lot provide the information."

"And get the credit?" Tony asked, arching an eyebrow.

My initial reaction was to get my back up, my ego offended at the idea. But I'd come to terms with the fact that first reactions were based on old habits. I planned to retire. What did it matter to me if my involvement went unrecognized? "Sure."

"And Barrett, you'll be working with her?"

Red floated in my vision, and I bit down hard to hold back the tirade brewing on my tongue. Was he seriously insinuating he wouldn't pass the hunt off if Barrett didn't stand as my watcher?

"I will," Barrett said.

Tony nodded. "I'll talk to my superiors and see what they say. If they don't have an issue, we'll pass along whatever information or tools we can. Weapons, locations, reinforcements—we have it all."

As far as deals went, it wasn't awful. Mikhail would be hard-pressed to gain much of a foothold with so many people closing in on him. And it beat having to work around the witch hunters. Or with them directly. I didn't think I'd be able to hold back from throwing a fireball into this guy's face if I had to spend any more time with him.

I clapped my hands together. "Wonderful. Great chat. We'll be in touch. Come on, Barrett. If you're ready to go, that is."

He met my eye, and I swore I caught a glimmer of amusement swirling through those inscrutable dark brown irises. He stepped to the side and gestured towards the door. "After you."

10

Katerina

WE PARKED IN front of Rune the Day, a glitzy storefront in the middle of commercial Bloor Street, around ten thirty that evening.

Barrett had said nothing about the open window the whole drive over, and I couldn't tell if his teeth were clenched from cold or annoyance. Either suited me. After the conversation with Tony, I was in no mood to play nice.

The shop was located between a Caribbean restaurant and a 3D-printing place and stood out like an overly glittered thumb. Decorative fencing barred the bottom half of the large picture window, but the effect was rustic and inviting rather than intimidating.

Through the window, I could see the store offered the usual fare—crystals and tarot cards, books on the craft. While most of it was your standard novice equipment, waves of stronger, darker magic prickled my skin from the back of the shop.

Not surprising, of course. If customers or employees of this store were following Mikhail, it made sense their tastes ran towards blood and death, but it meant I'd have to keep my eye on them.

Or I wouldn't. Because I was retiring.

The sign on the door was flipped to closed, but lights were on in the room behind the counter to the left side of the shop.

A private late-night reading?

A coven meeting?

Mikhail himself?

I wasn't about to let a lock get in my way. "Journey round back?"

To Barrett's credit, he didn't argue with me. I'd half-expected him to suggest we come back tomorrow, which would have lost us valuable time.

It took us a while to track down the alley that led to the back door, and I was pleased to find this door unlocked, supporting my suspicions that there were people inside.

"So here's how tonight is going to go," I said. "I'll go in and see what all the fuss is about. You'll stay upstairs to catch anyone who tries to run out. If you're able to stop them, great, but unless it's Mikhail, I don't think you need to get your hands dirty. If I'm not back in ten minutes, call Adrian and let him know I've been killed in a pathetic and ignoble manner that should in no way be spread through the magical circles because it would be way too embarrassing for my reputation. Underst—Barrett?"

The son of a bitch was already making his way into the shop, patting his belt where I caught the glint of a knife at his hip. The way he checked his boot and his lower back, I guessed there was much more to him than met the eye.

Although I always associated Barrett with guns, him being the soldier type, he was smart enough not to have any on him tonight. Guns and magic didn't mesh well in close quarters, with damage inflicted more often on the wielder than the target. Knives were a safer bet, and the fact Barrett knew that gave me some insight into how he and Adrian spent their evenings.

With a grumble, I entered the shop behind him and held my hands at my sides, ready to summon my magic at the first sign of threat.

"I suppose this means you're coming with me, then?" I asked softly, not wanting my voice to carry.

He replied with the slightest of nods. "Adrian told me to stick close, so we work together. If you want to play cowboy, that's your choice, but I won't allow your arrogance to let this witch slip away from us if we're able to stop him."

I opened my mouth to reply, but let it go. His condescending tone aside, the man was right. Against most magic users, I could take the upper hand, but Mikhail had escaped me twice. I couldn't afford to be cocky.

I also couldn't be distracted by having to keep Barrett safe, so I hoped he was prepared to take care of himself.

"If it comes to a fight, be ready to dodge their potion vials," I said softly. "If you don't have time to get out of range, raise your arm. Better to get splashed on a limb than your face. Cross your fingers they don't have time to cast any spell circles."

"I do have some experience against witches," Barrett grumbled.

We crept through the shop. The streetlights and traffic through the front windows lit our way towards the room behind the counter. But when I nudged the door open with my foot, I was surprised to find a stairwell instead of a stock room. The steps led down, and voices drifted towards us from the basement.

Chanting.

Definitely some kind of coven meeting, then.

Anticipation buzzed over my skin at the thought that we might track Mikhail down tonight and be done with it. The fight would be tricky, and no doubt painful, but if we were able to corner him, we stood a good chance of success.

My excitement ebbed as I assessed the power.

Strong, as one would expect it to be from multiple witches, but not nearly strong enough for Mikhail to be among them.

I looked to Barrett and shook my head. He nodded his chin towards the stairs, a question in his eyes, and I hesitated. We needed to speak to the witches who owned this store to learn about the people I'd found dead in that office building, but without knowing what they were up to, we could be walking into trouble.

What decided me was that until I saw it with my own eyes, I couldn't be sure Mikhail wasn't with them. If we left or waited for them to finish, the situation could become a hundred times worse.

So I nodded and led the way down the stairs.

The hum of magic grew stronger as we descended, making the hair on my arms dance. Instinctively, I reached for my own magic, letting flames run circles around my fingers, ready to launch it at the first provocation.

A stair creaked behind me. I glared at Barrett over my shoulder, but his focus remained solidly ahead, once more shaming me with his good thinking.

Noise was bound to happen, but we were far more likely to be taken unaware if we paused to look around than if we paid attention. Overcautiousness could be just as dangerous as not being cautious enough.

Boy, was I out of practice.

The voices grew louder, reaching us from across the basement. The open space of their stockroom was empty, but at the other end of the room was a doorway. By the cadence of the chant coming from beyond, the spell currently in progress was nearly at its crescendo. Perfect timing to pop in and say hi.

Once again, temptation whispered in my ear to lead with my magic. To throw open the door and charge in, fire blazing, but I forced the urge down and approached quietly.

I hadn't spent much time learning witchcraft, so for all I knew, they were performing a simple incantation for health and wealth. It would be rude of me to break down their door for something so innocent.

Even if a note of their magic did leave a nasty taste at the back of my mouth.

Wrangling my impulses, I shooed Barrett to the side and rapped a cheerful knock on the door.

Then dove out of the way as the door blew off its hinges into the stockroom.

Good to know my instincts hadn't disappeared completely.

I summoned my fire and let it creep up my arms, the runes set in my gloves helping me keep my power contained. The flames hugged the leather, spitting sparks into the harsh incandescent light. As soon as another spell flew my way, zipping past my left ear, I returned the volley with one of my own, launching a nickel-sized fireball into the room.

Screams of surprise reached me, and I crossed the threshold with more fire dancing over my hands. Exhilaration tingled through my blood, the long-forgotten thrill of the fight.

Seven witches stood inside, four of them wearing satchels I suspected were full of ready-made potions.

Did they always perform their rituals armed?

If so, I could probably kiss my health-and-wealth spell theory goodbye and we'd be having a bigger conversation.

A glass vial flew towards me and smashed against the wall beside my head. Shattered glass sprayed outwards, and a deep hole in the plaster smoked.

Not giving the witch a chance to launch a follow-up at me, I threw myself unreservedly into battle. I reversed my heat until frost covered my hands, then rested my palm against the wall. Frost bloomed around my fingers, trailed downwards, and cut along the floor in a stunning lace-work pattern.

Barrett ran in around me, blade in one hand, taser in the other. I'd missed that little device when I'd tallied his arsenal.

The frost climbed the legs of two of the nearest witches, trapping them to the concrete. I pushed harder, and it crept upwards until glittery white covered the backs of their hands. Then it thickened into ice and bound their arms to their sides, transforming them into half-melted ice sculptures in the middle of the room.

One of the witches threw a spell at Barrett's head, but he dodged and jammed the taser into her side. She convulsed and fell to the floor, but not before another witch reached into a pouch at his side and blew a handful of powder into Barrett's face.

Barrett wrenched his head away, but not in time, and the blisters bubbling over his cheek told me someone had been playing with substances the witch hunters had banned more than a decade ago.

"Tsk, tsk." I drew on my heat, formed a fireball in my palm, and threw it at the witch's pouch.

It caught fire, the flames flickering green, purple, and gold, and the witch shrieked as he worked to detach the pouch from his belt. I winced in empathy as the pouch burst and his screams filled the room.

A fifth witch tried to sneak around me, but I summoned another fireball at the same time Barrett threw his blade. It caught the shoulder of the woman's heavy sweater and pinned her to the wall.

As I drew more magic into my palms, I felt the first drain on my power. Already, I was running on empty.

The other two witches had pushed themselves into the corner, seemingly too terrified to engage with us. I pegged them as our weak links.

But when I moved towards them, they exchanged a glance, and in unison spoke a chant that made my skin vibrate as their magic surged towards me in the shape of a glowing circle marked with runes.

It took a lot of power to create a spell circle, even tag-teaming it as these two were. No wonder Mikhail had his eye on this coven.

Not sure I had the strength left to fend off the incoming magic, I dove to the floor beneath the circle. It hit the wall, shooting lightning bolts throughout the room. A stray bolt struck one of the witches who'd cast the spell in the chest. Her partner cried out, too focused on the death of her friend to notice Barrett before he tackled her to the ground.

I rose on shaking legs and brushed the dust off my knees.

Two witches frozen to the floor, one pinned to the wall, one recovering from being tased, one burned and cowering, and one trapped under Barrett. Only one dead, and not by my hand.

All in all, not a bad day.

For me.

As for the survivors… well. They'd pissed me off, so their day was about to get much worse.

11

Katerina

WHILE BARRETT WRESTLED with the witch underneath him, I summoned my fire and melted the ice around the two witches stuck to the floor. They glowered at me as they worked feeling back into their limbs, but I gave as good as I got.

"Here's the deal." I grabbed them both by the arms and shoved them against the wall next to the woman pinned with the knife. "We're here because I stumbled across some of your buddies dead in an office building." I pulled out my phone, opened it to the picture I'd taken of the dead man's face, and showed the one stuck to the wall. "Know him?"

She narrowed her eyes at me for a good long while. Unfortunately for her, I was a master at playing statue. When she finally accepted my superiority, her attention shifted to my phone, and the rest of the blood drained from her freckled face.

"That's Todd. Oh my goddess, that's Todd."

Her pallour turned a sickly shade of green, and I jerked the knife free so she could vomit in the corner instead of on my shoes.

I nodded at the witches previously encased in ice. "If you have anything in your satchels that'll help with her shock, I give you permission to use it.

Attack me, and you'll pay for it."

The man scowled but didn't hesitate to go to his crying, retching friend. I looked to the woman. "There were two more witches with him. Cut up like animals. Covered in blood, with the rest of their blood missing. Who wants to tell me what they were involved in?"

I scanned each person, taking in their micro-expressions and body language, working to figure out who would be the first to snap.

But their gazes had shifted to the woman trapped beneath Barrett.

Their leader, then. Good enough.

"Everyone against this wall." I summoned a fireball and let it hover over my fingers. "Satchels on the floor in front of me, and if I catch any of you reaching for some sneaky potion vial, you'll wish you were dead. Ask your buddy over there." I jerked my chin towards the man still gasping as he stared at the fabric melted into his skin. Someone was in for a long night in the ER.

While the other witches followed my orders and tossed their potion bags at my feet, the woman under Barrett was putting up quite a stink. She attempted to launch more spells to free herself from the soldier's weight, but he and Adrian had clearly practiced how to subdue a witch. He held her hands out of reach of her red-tasseled satchel and far from her hair or anything else she might use as a focal point. She'd had to team up with the dead witch to make her spell circle work, so if all she had was her potions, there wasn't much she could do to him.

I crouched beside her and cocked my head to look the woman in the eye. "What's your name?"

She spat at me, but I didn't flinch. If she thought a little saliva would be enough to chase me away, I judged the intelligence of their coven in naming her leader.

I grabbed her by the chin with my non-flame-bearing hand and drew on my fire. Heat soaked through my fingers into her flesh, enough to warm, not enough to burn. "Name."

She clenched her teeth, and I raised the temperature.

Barrett cast me a cautious look, the intensity of his expression lessened by the blisters around his squinting eye, but I ignored him. If he didn't like how I did business, he was welcome to leave me to it and go home. To paraphrase his words before we came in: I wasn't about to let compassion be the reason Mikhail escaped.

After I raised my heat another degree, the woman shouted, "Raisa!"

I let her go. "All right, Raisa, it's nice to meet you. What were Todd and these other two doing with Mikhail?"

Silence descended on the room, and the heaviness of it confirmed my suspicions that I'd pinned the correct blood witch. I looked to the man I'd frozen and found him glowering at me. Torn Sweater's eyes were wide open, as though my words had struck fear through her heart. Burning Man, Ice Woman, and Taser Lady kept their gazes trained on Raisa, but I sensed the tension emanating off them like a bad smell.

Raisa glared at me, hesitated a moment, then said, "A spell."

I couldn't help but laugh. "Obviously. What kind of spell?"

"Let me up and I'll tell you."

The challenge in her eyes was refreshing after the terror in everyone else's, and despite my desire to thump her over the head and speak with one of the witches cowering in the corner, I nodded at Barrett to release her.

He patted her down from head to toe, then removed the satchel that contained her potions and crystals and threw it into the pile with the others. Only after it was out of her reach did he give her space to stand up.

She used the wall for stability as she wobbled to her feet. Once standing, she crossed her arms and resumed glaring at me.

I mirrored her position and expression. "All right, you're standing. Now talk. Mikhail. What is he up to and where can I find him?"

Raisa scanned the other witches in the room—looking for approval? Permission? Whatever it was, she must have found it, because she gave a sullen shrug. "Something life-changing. That's what he said. Something that'll raise our power beyond what we could ever imagine. If something happened to Todd, he must not have been strong enough to handle it."

Something life-changing, indeed.

If Rhys's visions were anything to go by, that *change* would be an ending for these people. Mikhail would drain their power before he shared any with them.

"You don't care that your friend is dead? What about the others? Aside from Todd, are there any coven members who haven't shown up to your meetings lately?"

Torn Sweater sobbed. "Gary and Marlin. They haven't replied to any of my texts. I was going to swing by their apartment tomorrow if I hadn't heard from them tonight."

"Would you say they were strong?" I addressed the question to all of them but found myself focusing on Ice Man.

He shrugged. "I would have thought so if Mikhail chose them for his spell, but obviously not. He warned us of the risks."

I shoved my fingers through my hair and reminded myself they were mortal. Human. Prone to making horrible errors in judgement. Seriously bad. Terrible for the world bad. But that was my problem with witches. When the opportunity popped up for more power, too many of them took it, regardless of the consequences. There was no point in asking why. "Where is he?"

Again the others deferred to Raisa, whose contempt hadn't subsided. "We have no idea. He hasn't been around lately."

I drew in a breath and prayed for patience. "Those bodies were fresh.

You're telling me he rang up your buddies and off they went without telling anyone?"

"Of course. When someone like Mikhail invites you to work with him, you don't say no and you don't make him wait."

I bit my tongue to stop the curses bubbling up the back of my throat. Of all the naive, short-sighted…

"Do you have any idea when he planned to contact you next?"

More glowers, and I drew in another calming breath. I would not light her on fire. I *would not* light her on fire.

But it wasn't my magic that caused Raisa to go pale. Her gaze shifted over my shoulder, and I glanced back at Barrett, who stood behind me twirling his knife around his finger and catching the grip. An impressive skill to show off while delivering an unspoken threat. Raisa's throat bobbed with a hard swallow.

"There's an event—a masquerade—tomorrow night at the art gallery. He invited us all to come. Told us to dress nice and be ready to mingle. None of us could afford the tickets."

What was with Mikhail and art galleries?

I stepped closer to Raisa, and for the first time since we'd entered the room, her eyes widened with uncertainty. She retreated until her back pressed against the wall.

"Do you know who I am?"

She sneered, but it lacked the heat of her earlier rage. "You're the bitch who keeps us from becoming everything we could be."

She wasn't wrong, so I didn't argue with her. Had she ever witnessed a witch who'd gone too far? Grown bloated and wild on too much power? It wasn't pretty. So sure, I'd be generous and save her that fate.

"Since you know what I'm capable of, you'll do me a favour in exchange for walking out of here without taking a closer look at your inventory, won't you?" I asked.

Her gaze dipped to the satchels on the floor before it returned to meet mine, and she nodded.

"You'll let us know when he contacts you."

I pulled my card from my pocket and flipped it through my fingers to offer it to her. She hesitated before taking it. What did she think it was going to do? Explode?

"We're looking to speak with him about these big plans of his."

"Sure," she said. "As soon as he calls me, I'll let you know."

I couldn't help the snide smile that slid onto my face. "Of course you will."

And my name was Don Quixote.

Slowly, I backed away from her. "Thank you very much for your time. Have a wonderful rest of your evening."

Raisa's shoulders relaxed the more distance I put between us. I caught her hand reaching for her pants pocket, but before she had a chance to come at me, I flicked my fingers at her, releasing the fireball I still had floating over my palm. The potion vial exploded, smoke puffed into her face, and she collapsed to the floor in a slump. Her chest rose and fell, and I hoped for her sake that whatever had been in the vial would wear off eventually.

I turned on my heel to face Ice Woman. "You'll want to get your people checked out. Those burns on your guy over there probably hurt like a son of a bitch. And I recommend you tell your coven leader it's in her best interests to keep her promise. The longer you follow Mikhail, the more likely you are to see your last days."

Without a backwards glance, I headed out the broken door. Barrett refused to turn his back to them until he was clear of the doorway, and we both headed upstairs and out the back door into the frigid February night.

"You good?" I asked him.

"It's a few blisters, I'm fine. What now?" By the faint tic in his jaw, I guessed he wasn't happy.

"Now we go shopping," I said. "We have a gala to attend tomorrow night, and I have absolutely nothing to wear."

12

Katerina

BY THE TIME we returned to the car, Barrett had buried his feelings under his usual mask of stoicism. Even so, I sensed his displeasure like the vibrations in the air before a big storm.

I debated ignoring it.

I wasn't thrilled with how tonight had gone, either, but we'd gotten some good information and, if we worked smart, we'd have a chance to catch the witch tomorrow night. My first real chance in decades. Sure, Raisa would probably call Mikhail and let him know we were closing in, but we had room to manoeuvre.

Unfortunately, I was stuck with Barrett until Adrian called him home, and the last thing I needed was for his grumpiness to bump against mine. I would exhaust myself keeping him out of my emotional bubble.

Wanting to govern the terms of whatever lecture was coming, I opted to break the silence as I pulled my car door open. "What's up, Barrett?"

His jaw flexed, his anger not as under wraps as I'd thought.

"Are you going to make me guess?" I asked. "I can. I've gotten pretty great at twenty questions over the years. Was it the dismount? Because I agree, the landing could have been smoother."

"One of those witches died tonight," he growled as he wrenched open the driver's side door and dropped into his seat.

I blinked at him. Of all the things he might have been angry about, I was amazed that was where he'd focused. I settled into the passenger seat. "Her spell backfired."

The look he threw at me as he started the car might have frozen my blood if I weren't able to channel so much fire.

"What?" I asked. "Should I have shoved her out of the way and taken the hit myself? She knew the risk of casting it."

"That's exactly the problem with magic, isn't it? All these people throwing around power they don't know what to do with, while the few people who do know what they're doing stand by and do nothing."

"Excuse me very much?" I turned in my seat to face him. My skin prickled as I wrestled with my rising blood pressure. This attitude right here was why I disliked the man so much. "Here I thought I'd travelled hours away from my home to track down a brutal dark witch before he kills anyone else. My bad."

His nostrils flared, and I tapped my fingers against the windowsill. "Short of attacking them myself, there's nothing I could have done to stop them. I've seen it a thousand times. You heard them—they're head over heels for his lies. His promises of unlimited power." Away from the witches, I could finally roll my eyes, and it was satisfyingly sweet. "Please. No witch I know would promise anyone unlimited power. Everyone is out for themselves."

A truth I knew too well.

I also knew how badly those selfish ambitions could explode in one's face. After all, wasn't I still walking around when the three women who'd cast the immortality ritual were nothing but dust?

For a while, we drove in silence, both of us brooding, both of us annoyed with the other. The usual state of existence between us, but at least it was familiar. After the day I'd had syphoning information out of reluctant mouths with a narrow gasoline hose, I appreciated the chance to wind down with a task that required no effort.

"You really think they'll call us?" he asked after he turned onto Spadina. Only now did I realize he was taking us to Adrian's house in Kensington Market.

I barked out a laugh. "Not a chance in hell. They're more likely to call a meeting and try to hunt me down than they are to turn on Dear Leader. That's what he is, you know. He's got them thoroughly brainwashed to believe he's the be all and end all of witchy magic. The son of a bitch knows what he's doing. That's why he's so much of a threat. A lot of the time, the people who are too big for their britches have really tiny britches. Mikhail... well, his pants might just fit."

Barrett scowled, and I wasn't sure if it was at me, Mikhail, or the situation, but as far as I was concerned, at least two out of the three were warranted.

Nothing about the meeting tonight had gone the way I'd wanted it to—the way it might have a few centuries ago when I was at the height of my power. There was a time Raisa would have peed herself at the sight of me and jumped to tell me everything, knowing I was the scariest bitch to cross her path in this lifetime.

Instead, she'd scorned my power and was falling at Mikhail's feet for all his empty promises.

Over the past hundred years, I'd gone from being the guardian of the magical world, the avenging angel, mistress of the elements, to simply Kat Palon, sorceress. If I'd had any doubts of the change, that witch had made it pretty damned clear.

When I'd first become aware of my energy fizzling out, I'd tried to convince myself it was a temporary lull. That all I needed was time and I'd bounce right back.

But time was a greater bitch than I was, as I'd learned often enough.

My power had begun to wane around the point I realized that every time Emrick protected me from some danger or another, he sacrificed pieces of his soul. He'd lost enough of them that he'd begun to fade, little by little losing bits of himself. Too far down that path and he'd be nothing more than a wraith, with nothing remaining of the man I loved. So I'd stepped back from the hunts, allowed Adrian to take a greater role, and by doing so had caused blocks to grow around my magic. But even then, Emrick had always been there, involving himself in the mortal world for my benefit. Crossing boundaries he was forbidden to cross.

How many times had he promised to stay away? Yet every time I needed help, there he was.

In the end, I'd ordered him to leave my side, but it turned out he was the only thing holding my broken soul together. Without him, eternity had opened up before me like a vast, empty chasm, swallowing more of my magic.

For a while, I'd been too embarrassed to delve into the why. I'd tried to push through the barriers and failed until, eventually, I'd stopped trying. Not long after that, Adrian had retired, leaving me to trudge a path that no longer held any novelty or joy.

Now my once world-renowned power was as reliable as a beater car. Mikhail was probably having a good laugh at my expense.

Still, I reminded myself, we hadn't walked away empty-handed. We had our next step. A small but gentle consolation.

Barrett pulled up in front of the house and turned off the engine. I prepared to let myself out of the car when he said, "Tonight was…"

He trailed off, a deep furrow forming between his eyebrows.

"Impressive?" I suggested. "Wicked? A radical display of my skill and prowess?"

"Anticlimactic."

I blinked. "Excuse me?"

He shrugged and checked his side mirror, not even doing me the courtesy of meeting my eye as he insulted me.

"I've heard the stories of Katerina of Palonia. The woman who's taken down dark witches and demons and all manner of magicals. The woman who's helped keep mundanes in the dark about magical existence for nearly a millennium. Yet in that room, your abilities were… well, they just were."

His accusations fractured the effects of my pathetic little pep talk, giving them extra punch. Rage spiked in my blood, and I curled my palms in my lap to contain the fire that spread over my fingers. Heat spread up my arms, and I was glad the leather gloves were in place to filter my fury. The last thing we needed was for the car to go up in flames. Then we'd have to wait for transportation, find a shop, get a replacement… all of which would require spending more time together. And at the moment, all I wanted was to get away from this man who deigned to look down his nose at me.

I didn't need anyone else's judgement. My own was quite enough.

"You know what? Fuck off, Barrett. You don't know anything about me or my abilities. What would you have preferred? That I went full sorceress and burned the entire street to its foundations? Because I could have fucking done that."

It would have taken a while, and my magical reserves would have been tapped out for a few days, but I could have.

His eyes narrowed, and his hands tightened ever so slightly around the steering wheel. "I'm not talking about any show of strength. If anything, that's my point. You didn't think anything through. You gave no thought to what might be behind the door. You walked in as if you believed you could take on whatever it was. It was thoughtless, rash, and unprofessional. If I weren't here under Adrian's orders, I would drop you off and return to Muskoka. No one in their right mind would want to partner with someone who acts like she wants to get herself killed."

His face shut down, signalling the end of his tirade, and while I would have loved to keep going, to retaliate with every insult that came to mind, I turned towards the window and swallowed my anger.

Because to a point, he was right.

Yes, I wanted to stop Mikhail. I wanted to stop him from carrying out whatever he'd needed those witches' lives for, and I was willing to throw myself into the fight if it meant getting the chance to take him down.

But the fact was I wouldn't have died tonight.

I wasn't likely to die tomorrow.

I was doomed to keep putting one foot in front of the other until Death finally released Emrick from his obligations or I found a way to break the bond that tied me to the man who'd shaped my immortal life.

And as detached as I felt from the world, as uncertain as I was about my future, I wasn't ready for my life to end.

For whatever reason, a glimmer of hope remained that the dark cloud over my head would clear and I'd find a new way forward. That Adrian would leave his retirement. That Emrick and I might find a way to be together.

I'd been around long enough to know we couldn't reverse time… but I also knew how often history repeated itself.

As long as that glimmer remained, Barrett's words were unfounded, even if the thoughtless and rash part were often all too true.

I had made up my mind to go after Mikhail, and whether Barrett believed in me or not, I would find a way to end him.

13

Katerina

THE SOFT LIGHTS of the art gallery hit the wet sidewalk outside.

It had taken Tony's resources to narrow down exactly which art gallery was hosting the event, but we'd found out with enough time to get our tickets and make a very hasty, very shoddy, very desperate plan.

Barrett had accused me of being rash, so this time I made sure he took half the credit. As we'd sat down and cobbled together our expectations for the evening, he and I had agreed on a few key elements:

First, that if Mikhail had already completed one test run, he wouldn't wait long for another, larger, rehearsal.

Second, that this gala offered our best opportunity to take him down before anyone else died, even if it did mean pinning our success on hopes and luck.

And third, that it was too disturbing for Barrett and me to agree on anything, and we would be happier if it never happened again.

So here we were, both of us prepared to ad-lib our way through the evening, but only one of us able to appreciate the silver lining—the elaborate costumes.

I adjusted the lacy black cat mask on my nose and tied the silk ribbon under my pinned-up hair.

"Meow." I swiped my fingers at Barrett and refrained from laughing as he tied on his blue-and-purple peacock mask.

He looked miserable, and his misery added a brightness to my otherwise dark outlook.

Our costumes were a mix of custom and off-the-rack and one hundred per cent beautiful. Mine was a floor-length gown of crushed red velvet, with a cowl neckline and black lace sleeves that ended in a point and looped around my middle finger. The design meant I'd had to leave my gloves at home, but I'd make do. A bit less control over the direction of my magic was worth maintaining the gorgeous look of this dress. The skirt hugged my hips and flowed around my legs, with a slit that ran up the left side to mid-thigh.

I felt decadent. How long had it been since I'd enjoyed the chance to play dress-up?

Barrett, despite his gloomy face, looked strikingly handsome. The deep blue-green suit brought out the golden undertones of his dark skin and made his brown eyes vibrant. The seams highlighted his broad shoulders, emphasizing his impressively straight posture, and the purple cummerbund showed off the sleek lines of his hips and waist.

I was sure Adrian would be disappointed not to see him in this get-up, but Barrett had refused to let me take a photo.

"Do you want to run through the plan again?" I asked as I stepped out of the car. Barrett was by my side a moment later, handing the keys to the valet. "Or do you trust that I was paying attention?"

"Even the best plan benefits from repeated review." His gaze jumped between the people passing by us, not once settling on me. He was still pissed about how things had gone last night. That was fine. Our plan did not rely on us having to spend much time together.

"We go in, split up, find Mikhail," I said. "Even if he makes us—which is probable—I doubt he'll cause a scene with so many people around. Regardless, we don't make a move until he leaves. When he does, we grab him. If he has anyone with him, ignore them. Stay focused on the target and be prepared for potions and verbal spells. The goal will be to get control of his hands. Without them, there's not much he can do. He won't make it easy. Once we have him restrained, we head to the house where we dispatch him quickly and quietly with no further fuss. Am I missing anything?"

"It's an awful plan," Barrett grumbled, more stating a fact than with any heavy judgement.

"Any suggestions for last-minute improvements? Pull the fire alarm and hope the organizers reschedule for another night to give us more time to prepare? You've already vetoed me setting him on fire in the middle of the party."

I still held it would be the fastest way to deal with him. Not to mention we might get paid for providing entertainment. Win-win.

Barrett pressed his lips into a thin line, and I knew he had nothing.

Backup would have been nice, but the witch hunters hadn't been available on such a tight schedule. For better or worse—probably worse—we were on our own, and we'd have to work with what we had.

Our alternative was following the trail of corpses until we got another opportunity.

"All right, then," I said, offering my arm. "Shall we?"

Barrett ignored my arm, hooked my hand under his elbow, and escorted me towards the entrance.

Thank goodness for having contacts in this city, or we would never have been able to con our way into the masquerade. Marketed as a cultural fundraiser, the actual purpose of the evening was to raise money for the League of Magical Freedom. While I wasn't opposed to any group that kept the witch hunters in check, I'd been paying attention to its leaders for the past few decades as a potential future problem.

The tickets had been hard enough to come by, but with a big enough purse and a few promised favours—for the tickets and the seller's discretion—we'd managed to arrive fashionably late.

The decor was bright and tasteful, the lighting complimentary to all the costumes covered in sequins, jewels, feathers, and furs. Everyone dressed to the height of absurdity, oozing in wealth and power.

There was a reason I didn't dip often into my extensive bank accounts to spend on lavish occasions. They were filled with people I didn't enjoy spending time with, rich food, and wine with high price tags and low taste.

The people-watching, though. That made it worthwhile as a rare indulgence.

Barrett stuck close to my side as he showed the people at the door our tickets. They scanned them and waved us in, their attention already on the next people in line.

There must have been three hundred guests already inside, the colours a swirling kaleidoscope as they wound their way through the crystal-dominated space—vases on pedestals against the walls, glass chairs lined up between them, crystal flutes and matching serving dishes on trays.

One wrong step, and the entire room would shatter.

No wonder Barrett walked with his arms tucked so tightly to his sides. Or maybe he was keeping his hand close to the taser hidden under his jacket.

"If Mikhail is here, he should be easy to find," I said as I tipped my head at a man giving me a second glance. "Look for the most pretentious costume, and I suspect that'll be him."

Barrett grunted. "How will we decide what the most pretentious costume is?"

I chuckled and released his arm. "Happy hunting."

I left him to mingle on his own while I made my way to the far end of the room, flowing through the crowd as though it didn't exist. Experience helped me avoid elbows that popped out of exuberant conversations, and I took note of every face I passed.

So far, there was no sign of the blood witch, though I did recognize a few other people beneath their less concealing masks. High ups in the Ontario covens. A few from the European factions as well, which I found interesting. I didn't know if their attendance tonight had anything to do with Mikhail's plans, but I hoped it was just coincidence. It wouldn't matter if he killed them or recruited them, the diplomatic nightmare would be as much a headache to clean up as whatever he was planning.

I grabbed a glass of sparkling wine as the server passed by with his tray and found a place against the wall where I had a good view of the room. Soon enough I'd need to go and make small talk if I didn't want to draw attention to myself, but for the time being I soaked in the noise and bustle of the party.

Barrett should have thanked me. Some of these costumes were so extreme we could have taken ours up a few notches and still been understated.

A floral scent that struck me as familiar wafted beneath a spicy cologne as someone took the wall space beside me. "So many people showing their support for the magical cause."

I held back from rolling my eyes at the poor attempt at small talk, but my derision evaporated when I turned to look at the man who'd spoken.

He was leaning back against the wall, one foot propped up beneath him. One hand held a glass of sparkling wine; the other he held out towards me.

I tracked the hand up the arm, over the shoulder, to the face visible under a blood-red domino. So close to the colour of my dress, I might have sworn we'd coordinated on purpose.

Beneath the mask, a pair of black eyes glittered with amusement and no small amount of malice.

"Dance with me, sorceress?" Mikhail asked.

I set my half-empty glass on the table, not mourning the loss of the bland swill—proof that cost was no guarantee of quality—and accepted. As my fingers settled in his palm, I was grateful he wore gloves. Even through the cloth, the flow of his magic prickled my skin and raised the hair on the back of my neck.

I tamped down the power that threatened to rise in response to his and followed him to the centre of the room, where brightly coloured couples were taking the first steps of a waltz.

It had been years since I'd danced, and I hated that my first partner after so long should be a man I longed to burn to cinders in the middle of this crowded room. Curse Barrett and his veto.

By the smile teasing Mikhail's lips, he knew where my thoughts had gone.

"I heard you've been looking for me," he said.

Of course Raisa had given us up. I'd expected it, but expectation didn't prevent disappointment.

His knowing we were here didn't change our plan—as pathetic a plan as it was. All it meant was we'd have to be prepared for a bigger showdown. My magic tingled in my fingertips. I wasn't about to let this opportunity slip past us.

"Not really," I said. "A man like you doesn't know how to keep a low profile. I knew it wouldn't take long to track you down."

"Now that you have, what do you mean to do with me?" He spun me and brought me back, surprisingly graceful for a demon-summoning butcher.

"I plan to find out what you're up to." I stepped back and then forward before he spun me again.

"And then?"

"And then I'll stop you."

He chuckled. "You've tried before, Ms. Palon. Many times. Your failure suggests either you're not strong enough to do it or you secretly want me to succeed." He canted his head to the side. "Why don't you join me instead? I have so much to offer my followers, but you—I could give you everything you desire."

A shudder rippled through me, but I hid it under a smile. "I appreciate the invitation, but I desire nothing more than to get in your way at every turn until I destroy you. I won't deny I've underestimated you in the past, but do you really believe I'll continue to do so?"

"I don't," he said, giving me one last spin. "I think you'll be at the top of your game." He dipped me low and set his lips close to my ear. "And I think you'll still fail."

He brought me back up and bowed over my hand. Then he went so far as to kiss the back of it. After all his manhandling, I would now have to burn this dress when I got home, which made me very sad.

"Enjoy the rest of your evening, Ms. Palon," he said, and walked away.

With no way of keeping him in place, I had no choice but to let him melt into the crowd. From the way he stayed within my line of sight as he made a tour of the room, he knew our intentions and was rubbing it in our faces. If I had to guess, he would make sure he stayed visible for the rest of the evening and make a big production of leaving so we'd have no choice but to walk into his trap if we didn't want to lose him.

Mikhail had shown nothing except his usual collected arrogance, but I hoped his knees were shaking. He should be afraid. He'd escaped me twice before, had already killed three witches, and had corrupted my beautiful costume.

Oh yes, I was coming for him. The rage running through me right now was nothing to the agony he'd feel before the end.

I scanned the room for Barrett and found him against the wall opposite me, standing near the snacks. Wise man. He met my eye, and I signalled towards Mikhail. Barrett nodded and stuffed another hors d'oeuvre into his mouth before he shifted his attention to our target.

We had from now until the minute Mikhail said his farewells to strengthen our approach, but unless Barrett suddenly developed magically warded skin and a wicked superpower, we were firmly in wing-and-prayer territory.

I'd been there before. Never fun, but I refused to call it impossible. As long as we were ready for anything to happen, we could pivot and face it.

As though the universe felt the need to test my theory, the temperature dropped and white mist spilled around my feet.

In another moment, Emrick stood before me, breathtaking in white and silver. A white shirt tucked into white pants were complemented with white gloves, while a silver vest and a matching silver mask brought out all the brighter shades of his silver eyes.

Where was the server with the alcohol when you needed him? At the rate my night was going, I'd drink the whole bar dry before I was finished.

14

Emrick

KATERINA WAS A vision in red.

The lace mask obscuring the top of her face made her ocean-blue eyes so much deeper and highlighted her painted lips in a way that made me want to claim them with mine.

My heart raced, my skin flushed, and I relished every sensation. I was walking Death, more spirit than man, but she made me feel alive in ways no one else ever had.

Without considering anything beyond my own wishes, I held out my hand, and the speed with which she accepted told me she'd responded out of centuries-old habit.

I tried to hide my smile as I pulled her towards me and set my hand on her waist.

Dipping my head towards her ear, I said, "Mikhail is here."

Goosebumps rippled over her bare neck as my breath whispered across her skin, but when she spoke, her voice was as sharp as barbed wire. "Oh, I know. He already added his name to my dance card."

A muscle in my jaw ticked. "In that case, I'll have to make sure I show him up."

The desire filled me to cross the room to where Mikhail stood watching us and turn him to dust.

I wouldn't, of course. Not only could Katerina solve her own problems, but she wouldn't appreciate me breaking my promise in doing it for her.

The press of her hips against mine as we fell into the opening notes of a slow foxtrot carried my memories back to other ballrooms, other musicians—all the way to the first time she and I had danced together some eight hundred years ago. How awkward we'd both been. How reluctant to admit or act on our growing feelings for each other.

Now those feelings were out in the open—had been acted upon countless times—yet in a way we were right where we'd started.

The greatest difference between now and then was how familiar she felt in my arms. How natural.

"You're not here to whisk me off to another crime scene, are you?" she asked, her nose crinkling.

"Not this time. I happened to be in the area. Thought I'd swing by and see how your evening was going."

She pressed her deliciously red lips into a flat line. "Mmhmm. Adrian asked you to keep an eye on me, didn't he?"

I forced my gaze up to meet hers. "He didn't have to. Not as soon as I knew Mikhail was involved." I looked over her shoulder to where the witch stood on the edge of the crowd watching her, his dark eyes like burning coals through his mask.

Her fingers tightened around my hand. "You haven't found more bodies, have you?"

"Not yet. But where he's concerned, you know they're coming. Be careful, Kat."

"I always am."

The response earned her a humourless laugh. My sorceress didn't know how to be careful. Not if there was trouble she could dive into.

"Please tell me you're not here to help." Suspicion mounted in her voice and in the sharpness of her gaze.

"Only watching," I promised. "Passing on what information I can."

Her eyes narrowed, as though she didn't believe me for a second.

I grinned at her skepticism, then enjoyed a thrill of satisfaction as longing spilled into her eyes. Though her desire was far from one-sided.

We wound through a few more steps in silence, muscle memory taking over as our thoughts travelled wherever they'd gone. Mine had settled on the last time we'd danced like this. Argentina in the early 1920s. A tango and a legion of lesser demons. Kat and I had torn through them as we danced, not once missing a step or taking our eyes off each other.

Once the music ended and the demons were dead, I'd transported her back to Switzerland where we were staying with Adrian and we didn't leave the bedroom for three days.

Her breath caught, her lips parted, and I realized my memories weren't the only part of me that had risen with the flow of our dance.

I cleared my throat and released her as the music ended.

"Stay away, Emrick," she pleaded, her voice so quiet I barely caught it over the crowd's applause for the musicians. "Trying to help will only do more harm than good."

I knew the potential of another fragment of my soul being stripped away tormented her. It bothered me, too. What would I lose? Another memory? The pigment in my hair? The changes were so subtle, I'd hardly noticed them myself when they first started, and neither of us knew how many more fragments it would take before the cost was my feelings for Kat. Before I was no longer Emrick but an Emrick-shaped wraith.

I scowled. "I won't leave you hanging out on a limb when that witch is involved. I can keep my distance, but only so far."

I'd seen how Mikhail had pushed her in the past. To the edge of despair if not of life. And the way he stared at her right now… he had plans for her.

Kat's expression turned sad. "You've sworn to keep your distance so many times I've lost count. Now look where we are."

Her words struck me as deep as a knife to the heart, but I couldn't argue with her. It was true. I'd broken my word a hundred, maybe a thousand times, but I couldn't bring myself to regret it.

As the music for the next song began, she turned away from me and disappeared into the crowd. I looked up and met Mikhail's eye. He smirked at me and raised his glass, then returned to his conversation.

Did he know what I was? Was he anticipating how busy he was about to make me?

I kept my eye on him as I stepped through the mist into the emptiness of the afterlife and towards the obligations that awaited me.

I wouldn't stay away, but I would be careful in how I proceeded. Despite what Kat seemed to think, I wasn't willing to risk everything I was—though a few pieces of myself were worth sacrificing if it meant Kat lived to breathe another day.

15

Katerina

My body was still singing with lust and longing when I noticed Mikhail slipping out of the party.

Despite the way he'd watched me since our dance, despite the way he'd acted as though he wanted to stay in view, I swore he was trying to escape me.

Interesting.

Giving him only a few seconds' head start, I followed him into a quieter, cooler hallway. A few people milled about, oohing and aahing over the artwork, but Mikhail was already out of sight.

Not wanting to lose him but not wanting to get too far without my only backup, I pulled up the layers of my skirt to grab the phone strapped to my thigh and texted Barrett.

Me: He's on the move. West exit.

I started down the hallway, searching for the route Mikhail might have followed. East would take him back towards the front entrance, and if he was trying to avoid me, I doubted he would be so obvious.

My phone buzzed.

Satan's BFF: On my way.

I spotted the red glowing sign over the door in the back corner. Although the sticker on the doors warned me this was an emergency exit only, someone must have deactivated the alarm because the door had been propped open with a brick. Likely by a few gallery employees looking to sneak out for a mid-evening smoke, but a great way for Mikhail to slip out as well.

Me: I think I have his trail. Open door. Catch up.

I returned my phone to my leg. It buzzed a few more times—no doubt Barrett telling me not to go on my own—but I ignored it. Barrett wouldn't be too far behind me, but if I didn't stay on Mikhail's heels, we might miss him.

Focused only on not losing this opportunity, I passed through the door into a loading bay. Aside from an emergency light above the door, the area was filled with shadows that stretched towards me, threatening to consume me if I didn't move.

It had been quite a few centuries since I'd been afraid of shadows.

Choosing to remain in the darkness, I kicked off my shoes—they'd been super uncomfortable, and I wasn't sad to lose them—removed my mask—a greater loss—and moved soundlessly along the pavement, keeping my eyes open for any sign that someone had come this way recently.

The ashy reek of cigarette smoke tickled my nose, and I scrunched my face to keep from sneezing. A breeze picked up and blew it away while bringing with it a hint of Mikhail's spiced cologne.

I picked up my pace and reached the corner. As I rounded it, I spotted the blood witch walking briskly towards a waiting car.

If he reached it, we'd lose our chance.

If I intercepted him, I'd be triggering an earthquake under our already shaky plan.

Fuck it. I couldn't watch him speed away and do nothing.

Striding forward, I summoned magic into my hands. Flames licked around my fingers and over the backs of my palms, catching the lace and spreading up my arms. I tore the sleeves off at the seams before the fire jumped to the rest of the dress.

Ideas flurried through my head on what I should do. Blow up the car? Blow up Mikhail? Tempting, but even at this hour of the night, there were too many people walking by for the burst of magic to go unnoticed.

When he sped up, I accepted that I'd run out of time. Making it up on the go it was.

I reversed my heat to extinguish my fire, pushed myself into a run, and in another moment I had him by the arm, ready with a hand covered in frost. I sent it creeping up his sleeve until it thickened and bound us together.

He snarled and tried to rip away, but my magic was too strong.

The driver's side door opened, and a man stepped out. I flicked a small fireball at him with my free hand. Not enough to injure, just enough to scare him back into hiding, which he promptly did. I sent another fireball at the car's front tire and watched the rubber melt onto the pavement.

"I would very much like it if you came with me, Mikhail," I said.

So I can kill you in private.

I left that part unsaid, but by the gleam in his dark eyes, he heard it anyway.

Rapid footsteps echoed on the sidewalk behind me, and I hoped it was Barrett and not more of Mikhail's people. To be safe, I pumped more fire into my empty hand and jerked Mikhail forward.

He hauled me back. "I don't think so, sorceress. But thanks for playing."

Barrett reached Mikhail's side, taser in hand, just as Mikhail smashed a vial against my face.

Glass shattered, and my skin sizzled under the effects of the potion. Smoke—fumes—whatever it was—ate away at my flesh, pinching my nerve endings. I swallowed my screams and renewed my concentration on my magic.

Too late.

Mikhail spun out of his jacket and threw himself at the car. Barrett leapt on him, and Mikhail's body jerked as the force of the taser powered through him. He slumped to the ground, and Barrett stepped back to get a grip on his arm. Through my watery eyes, I spotted the driver getting out of the car again, potion vial in hand.

I threw another fireball, and it caught the vial in a blast of purple flame, but the guy had come prepared. Four more vials flew from his other hand, and I couldn't move fast enough to block them all.

The driver had been smart and targeted Barrett over me. I would heal if I got hit—Barrett might not.

Without giving myself a chance to second-guess my actions, accepting what I was giving up, I threw myself at Barrett and took him to the ground. Glass and magic fractured against my back, and this time I couldn't hold back a scream as they tore into me, fire and ice and acid.

A car door slammed, then another, and I rolled to the side in time to watch the driver make a bumpy getaway with an unconscious Mikhail in the passenger seat. They were moving slowly enough that I should have gone after them, but pain clouded my vision and I didn't have it in me yet to get to my feet.

I rolled onto my stomach and buried my head in my arms, breathing through the agony. The effects of those potions were going to hurt for a few hours.

"What the fuck was that?" Barrett growled.

"You're welcome," I wheezed against the concrete.

Once I caught my breath, I raised my head. Barrett was sitting up, braced on his hands. Next to him was one of the vials. The bottle was cracked at the top, but the rest of it was intact, and the label on the bottom bore a logo with the letters *P.L.*

Fire spread over the backs of my hands, and I pushed myself up so I could shake them out.

"We had him, Kat. Why did you let him get away?"

Barrett stood up, and by his glower and stern tone, I was in for another lecture. This one, however, I didn't deserve.

I grabbed the vial, lurched to my feet, and turned my back to him so he could see the state of my once beautiful gown. "It was a choice between you or him. I figured I would rather find another opportunity to stop him than have to explain to Adrian why you were missing half your face. If that was the wrong call, then I'm sorry."

As I turned back around, his expression went slack in horrified understanding. He shifted on his feet to stare in the direction the car had gone.

"We've just fallen to Plan B of following the trail of corpses, haven't we?" he asked.

"Maybe not." I scowled. Cold wind blew through the holes in my bodice thanks to splashes of Mikhail's potion. Good thing I'd already grieved the loss of this dress. "Thanks to someone's need for recognition, we have a lead that might help us get ahead of him again. First, I need to go home and change into something less tragic, then we have an errand to run."

"Oh?"

I closed my hand around the broken vial.

"I know where Mikhail's sourcing his potions, and if she sold them to him directly, I'll have to remind her how much she should fear me."

16

Katerina

BARRETT AND I stood at the bottom of the steps to Moon in Venus. The large gold-on-blue sign hung over the door with impressive tole-painted detail, and matching signs hung in the windows advertising the magic and mysteries found within.

Unlike Rune the Day, a store that catered to the more knowing of magic users, this shop appealed to the dabblers and tourists. Sweet, charming, innocent. After my run-in with Mikhail's arsenal, I had my doubts, but I had to give credit for appearances.

We'd gone home to change into more comfortable clothing—black sweater, black jeans for Barrett; black leather pants, black T-shirt, runed gloves for me—but had still made it here long before opening. In the early hours of the morning, dawn was taking its sweet time lighting the winter sky. Streetlights spilled pools of warm light down the length of the side-walk, but nothing brightened the steps leading to the glass front door.

Compared to the hum of traffic on the surrounding roads, this street remained eerily quiet, as though separated by an unseen barrier.

I caught Barrett scowling at the windows. "You know you don't have to be here with me. You could have stayed at the house."

"I don't know what you hope to accomplish making the same suggestion over and over. We're working this together as I was ordered."

He didn't come out and say he was especially motivated by my last two train wrecks, but I heard it all the same.

Or maybe that was me projecting my own disappointments.

Whatever the case, I didn't intend to fail again. Not until I had this little witch begging me for mercy if she had set a single potion in Mikhail's greedy palm.

"Fine, but whatever you hear, don't lose your shit, all right? You're going to get all disapprovey, but I know what I'm doing."

He narrowed his eyes, already ignoring my guidelines. In the end, he said, "Fine," and jerked his head towards the door that led to the apartment upstairs. "Should we knock?"

"No, I want to start in the shop."

He frowned. "Why?"

"Because it's been three years since I've seen her, and I want to know what she's involved in. If she's dealing with Mikhail, she's not about to confess it without a little prodding."

I started towards the shop door, but Barrett cut in front of me, leaving me to follow.

I scowled at his back and considered letting him try the door handle, just to see what would happen. Unfortunately, the thought of Adrian's reaction if I allowed his thrall to be hurt killed my fun, and I called for Barrett to wait before he made contact.

He looked over his shoulder with impatience, and I bumped him aside to lean closer to the door.

"Thought as much," I said. "If you'd touched this, you would be on the way to emergency with burned palms. It's caustic powder."

Barrett's eyes widened, and he took another look up at the windows—

at the *20% off* sign perched cheerfully on a shelf of commercial tarot cards and the *We Sell Agate* announcement over a collection of loose stones.

"How does your witch friend expect to get customers? Or at least keep them."

"It's a nightly ritual. By the time the door opens for the day, there'll be no trace of the stuff to catch the unwary. Though gods help you if you try to steal anything."

I used the outside of my T-shirt like a glove and opened the door, unsurprised to find it unlocked. Barrett followed me in and shut the door behind me, wisely keeping his hands on the panel of the door.

Once we were inside and away from any curious eyes, I drew heat down my arm and into my gloved hand until flames wrapped around my fingers and a small ball of fire hovered above my palm.

Barrett eyed me warily, his expression twisted in contempt. I ignored him and set the fireball hovering above me to light our way as we navigated the aisles.

Above the counter hung a sign that matched the ones above the door and in the windows, advertising love potions, tarot and palm reading, crystals, and other magical paraphernalia.

True to the sign's word, I was surrounded by props of the occult and magical. Glass display cases announcing sales on totems, jewellery, and clothing, athames crafted out of various stone and metals, crystal balls, bins of multi-coloured rocks—all of it beautiful and impressive, but mostly for show. No more useful than a flower on a bonnet.

Despite its theatricality, this place had managed to keep Madame Proserpine in business and living in downtown Toronto for a good number of years, so she obviously knew her clientele.

"Watch where you step and try not to touch anything," I said. "She's been known to keep all sorts of traps lying where you least expect them."

"Like that trigger on the floor?"

I glanced down and performed a quick, ungraceful hop to the right to avoid the small switch hidden against the floorboard. With a quick exhale, I forced a grudging, "Thank you."

Barrett brushed me aside with a light nudge of his elbow and trailed his fingers along a thin wire attached to the switch that led to a dull axe hanging on the wall.

"You wouldn't have died," he said, "but you'd have wound up with a pretty nasty dent in your skull."

As he worked to disable the trap, I stared at the blade. He wasn't wrong that it wouldn't have killed me, but the edge still looked mean.

"Then I'll thank you a second time," I said. "After so many years, I hold my undamaged skull very dear to my heart."

Barrett sniffed and lowered the axe to the floor, propping it against a bin of meditation CDs.

"Who is this Madame Proserpine, anyway?" he asked as we picked our way carefully towards the back of the store. "A witch, obviously, and one with dark interests. But that just makes me wonder why she's free to sell her crap and live comfortably above the store. Why haven't you dealt with her if she's such a problem?"

He looked around the section of more advanced, questionable magic, and held up what appeared to be a cat skull. His nose wrinkled in distaste. The skull was impressive to look at, but that was about it. I didn't sense any magic wafting off it, only what it had gathered sitting in a magical shop.

"She's able to sell these trinkets because I've already dealt with her. At least I thought I had. I tried to kill her a few years back."

A book called *Curses, Hexes, and Afflictions: Protection Spells for Darker Times* lay on the counter. I flipped it open, flicking through the pages.

"You failed?"

Maybe it wouldn't have bothered me so much if he'd sounded amused. It was the lack of surprise in the question that made me see red. As though I would have met his expectations by failing.

I slammed the cover shut. The fireball hanging over my head flared, piercing more shadows in the corners of the shop. "I opted for mercy. A few years ago, she was the associate of a known necromancer, someone I was hunting. She told me where to find Laila in exchange for her life." Small bins along the bottom of the back wall caught my attention, and my eyebrow quirked. "Of course, the other part of the bargain was that she behave herself, and I see she's gone lax on that one. A dangerous move considering she's on her last chance with me."

Moving behind the counter, I crouched down to pick through the organized herb packets. Belladonna, wolfsbane, and other well-known and not-so-well-known poisons. The shopkeeper was a naughty witch.

I took the book and a few packets with me, then led the way out of the shop and towards the door partially tucked behind some creeping vines. Unlike the shop door, the witch kept this one locked, and after a quick scan to ensure no other traps lay in wait for anyone trying to get in, I looked to Barrett. "Any thoughts?"

"Ringing the doorbell would probably be a good start," he said.

"And have her running down the fire escape to avoid us? Try again."

He let out a resigned sigh and dropped to one knee.

I brought my hand to my chest. "Oh my. Isn't this a little fast? Adrian would never approve."

The guy didn't bother to react—rude—before pulling a set of lockpicks out of his back pocket and setting to work on the door.

"Huh. Both you and Adrian failed to mention that particular skill."

"You'd have figured it out if you paid attention."

I made a face at his back, but some of my irritation faded when the lock clicked and he opened the door to a darkened stairwell. The narrow space was enclosed, with no windows and no light other than a strip coming from under the door at the top of the stairs. The wallpaper—peach with pink flowers—looked new. I suspected that when the witch first purchased the house, the ascent had less of a claustrophobic feel. No doubt she had put up the paper with the same motivation that had inspired the caustic powder and the axe—all the better to keep people away.

As we started up the stairs, the door behind us swung shut, leaving us in darkness broken only by the fire hovering above my palm.

"Did you hear that?" Barrett whispered behind me.

I stopped, strained my ears, but heard nothing other than the stifled silence of the stairwell.

"Sounded like hissing," he said.

Then I heard it. A rustling noise creeping up the steps behind us. We looked around, but I saw nothing except the wooden stairs and burgundy floor runner.

"It better not be a snake," Barrett grumbled. "I hate snakes."

"Unless it's in the walls, I think we're all right." Then I remembered whose house we were in, and my confidence waned.

Again the rustling, this time accompanied by a cold draft that whipped around my legs and crept under my shirt. Then nothing. And in the absence of wind and sound, the stillness in the corridor was even more constricting.

I was no stranger to the eerie, but the hair on my arms stood on end. With my awareness heightened, I picked up the subtlest sounds—my light step on the carpet and Barrett's near-silent tread. It occurred to me how strange it was for so large a man to make so little noise as he walked. No other sounds from the building made it into the stairwell, and even though I had just come in from outside, I could easily believe myself trapped in this angled, rectangular box.

A light floated past the corner of my eye. I froze, and Barrett bumped into me with a grunt. When I tried to follow the light, it disappeared.

"There," Barrett whispered, pointing straight ahead.

The light floated four feet off the ground in front of the apartment door, filling out until it resembled the shape of a human being. It shimmered like water but cast no shadow. No glare.

The light moved, stretched towards me like an arm, and as it came closer, fingers formed. Fingernails extended into claws, withered skin defining itself like lines in a sketch drawing. Wrinkles crept up the arm, the neck, and into what had become the spirit's face. Long, stringy hair spilled from its head and fell to its waist.

My stomach twisted, and I dropped the book and herbs to summon magic into my hands, though it wouldn't do much good against a spirit. Unlike a demon that might attempt to invade mind and body, spirits targeted only the mind, absorbing power to fuel their continued existence.

With the amount of power in my blood, the damned thing would be corporeal within minutes, ready to rampage across the city.

As for Barrett… well, his life force would make for a juicy appetizer.

Both arms reached for me now. The creature opened its mouth, a black chasm of nothing, and released a wail that left ice in my blood and stopped my heart. Behind me, Barrett backed away. I heard the doorknob jiggle, but the door didn't budge. Locked.

The cries invaded my mind, making it difficult to form a coherent thought, but I pushed through the cacophony and steeled myself against it.

Unable to get out through the bottom door, Barrett tried to push past me to get to the top. One of his blades was in his hand, but what he hoped to do with it against a figment of air and magic, I had no idea.

I did, however, know what the spirit would do to Barrett, so I grabbed his arm before he got too close and jerked him back.

A memory nagged at me, something Emrick had told me about spirits. Although my heart rebelled against playing it through, the adrenaline rushing through my veins pushed me head over heels into the past.

The warm crackle and glow of a fire, limbs entwined, fingers running through my hair with lazy sensuality, talking to pass the witching hour.

Watch for the fire in their eyes, he'd said.

"What do they look like?" I asked, tracing my fingertips over the coils of the wolf tattoo on his chest, enjoying the current of energy that buzzed under my skin at the contact.

"Who?"

"The spirits. Are they beautiful?"

Grandmother had put Kyla and me to sleep for years with tales of the trees and water, of the stones and wind, each with their own spirit to guide them, and here was a man who had seen them. Spoken to them. Guided them home.

"In their own way, I suppose they are. Not as beautiful as you, of course."

He nuzzled my ear, and I pushed him away with a laugh, then nestled closer against him. "Don't change the subject. Tell me what they look like."

He wrapped his arms around me, as though any space between us was an unspeakable crime. "They're strange. Like they're made of light that doesn't reflect on anything. They shimmer like water, but there's no substance to them. They can be tricky to find because they blend into their hosts, becoming the water or the wind or the bark. All the better to sneak up on their victims."

"How do you know what to look for?"

"You watch for the eyes," he said. "Eyes like fire, beautiful and terrible. If you see those eyes, you run."

"You don't run," I said, not liking his suggestion that I couldn't handle anything he could. I wasn't weak.

He laughed, his chest vibrating beneath my hand. "If they came at me, they'd wind up where they don't want to be. You? You'd make a delicious meal. Sweet and salty. So watch for those eyes."

The advice had been given partly in jest, but now I took it to heart and stared at the wailing creature. Hollow eyes stared back at me, sockets black and empty. Terrifying it may be, but it was no true spirit.

On a whim, I extinguished the fire in my hand, and Barrett disappeared into shadow. Only the figure before us remained visible. Without the flame, I made out something else, something faint, barely perceptible—a fine beam of light that caught on the dust motes floating through the air and made them sparkle. It led from the figure to a spot above the door.

In the dark, I reached for Barrett's hand and lifted it until it blocked the light. The figure disappeared.

"A projection," I said in my regular indoor voice. Whispers were for shadows and uncertainty, neither of which we faced.

Barrett snorted, though I could tell he was impressed. So was I.

Proserpine had developed some new tricks.

The wailing, once terrifying, now grated on my nerves.

I focused the fire back into my hand to light the stairwell, and Barrett scoured the wall for the mechanism to turn off both noise and projection. With a grunt of satisfaction, he moved closer to the left side of the door and rose onto the tips of his toes, his arm straining to get higher. He soon gave up and turned to me.

"I can't reach it. Come here, I'll give you a boost."

"What? I—"

He left me no time to protest. Gripping my waist, he hoisted me up to his shoulder. "You see the switch?"

I saw nothing until I moved my fireball closer and spotted a lump under the wallpaper. Not a lump, it turned out, but a light switch that had been wallpapered over. I hit it. The noise stopped, and the spirit faded.

"Thank the gods that's done," I said as Barrett set me down. "Let's see if we can wrap things up here without any more excitement, shall we? Though it's hard to see how she could top that."

Shaking off my adrenaline surge, I picked up the discarded book and herbs and headed up the stairs. The figure didn't return to batter my eardrums a second time.

I reached the door and breathed with relief to find it unlocked. The hinges creaked loudly, but after the noise of the fake spirit, I held no hopes of taking the witch by surprise.

Barrett and I moved out of the stairwell into the warm light of a cozy apartment, and there to greet us was the barrel of a gun aimed at my head.

17

Katerina

I BLINKED AT the gun, then rolled my eyes.

"Nice to know that when your elaborate plans fail, you can rely on the classics," I said.

"I can't always be sure my triggers will work, you know? Need some kind of backup. Damn it, kitty Kat, you couldn't have called?"

Proserpine Lister lowered the gun and set it on the end table beside a mint-coloured sofa. As she leaned over, her white satin robe fell open to reveal a coral lace-and-satin camisole that set off the rich notes of her skin and flaunted her ample curves. At Barrett's throat-clearing, she pulled the robe closed with talon-length red nails and grinned.

To look at Poppy wouldn't be to associate her with whoever had set up the intricate traps downstairs. Her large brown eyes, dark brown curls with pink tips that bounced past her shoulders, and well-manicured eyebrows gave the impression of a soft, innocent woman.

Very much in line with a shop owner of new age bits and bobs instead of the ambitious necromancer I knew her to be.

"Calling would have ruined the surprise," I said, moving past our awkward arrival. "Besides, I wouldn't have wanted to miss the upgrades to your shop. The ghost is an especially nice touch."

Her smile widened. "Just set it up last week. It's pretty wicked, right? You're the first to set it off. Goddess, it scared me. Might have to turn the volume down."

I shrugged. "Or leave it as is. Works better than a doorbell, and if your intruders make it through the door, they won't know which way is up."

Poppy's eyes sparkled, and she nodded towards Barrett. "Who's the quiet one?"

"This is Barrett. Barrett, Poppy."

One eyebrow lifted, but the rest of his expression remained neutral. "A necromancer named Poppy?"

Poppy's smile remained in place, but her hand twitched, and I wondered if she was thinking about the gun on the table. I knew a little of the story behind her name and how it had plagued most of her life. Named Proserpine by two driving forces in the witch community, she had grown up a bitter and angry child and taken the name Poppy as a less offensive replacement.

"I only use my full name on business cards. It's useful when you sell love potions." Calmed from the shock of our sudden visit, she took the time to knot her robe as she turned to me. "So what brings you here in the goddessforsaken hours of the morning? Just wanted to say hi?"

"Pretty much. We were at a party tonight. Ran into some people that made me think of you. Though maybe I should have stopped in sooner."

I held up the packet of nightshade I'd taken from downstairs.

Poppy waved a hand in dismissal. "That stuff? It's nothing. Most of those packets are full of cooking herbs. You're holding oregano right now."

"And this?" I asked, holding up the book.

She shrugged. "Mostly hooey. Curses and hexes written by hacks who don't know their agate from their bloodstone. But it sells."

She motioned for us to follow her, flipping a switch in the living room to cast a warm glow over the comfortable arrangement. The decor was a complete opposite from the gothic look downstairs, and as colourful as the woman who owned it. A large pink-and-cream area rug stretched over the hardwood floor, complementing the rosy paint on the walls. The easy chairs and sofa, all in matching mint green, sat around a gas fireplace with a good-sized television mounted above it. Unlike the store-owner Proserpine, there was no mystery to Poppy. She was a woman who enjoyed her comforts and, I knew, was willing to go to great lengths to keep them.

It was something we had in common.

Just in very different ways.

I sank into one of the easy chairs, crossed my legs, and rested my arms flat against the armrests. Barrett chose the bare wooden dining chair that he pulled up beside me. He sat and crossed his arms. His blatant refusal to be comfortable in the home of a magic user amused me.

Unfortunately, our reason for being here didn't allow me the luxury of poking him about it.

I looked around the room. "You're doing all right for yourself."

"I get by," Poppy replied, taking the chair across from me and tucking her feet under her. The hem of a pair of coral satin shorts peeked out from under her robe. "Why are you really here? As much as I love early morning chats with a woman who wanted to kill me, I don't believe you popped in to see an old pal."

I clasped my hands over my stomach and met Poppy's eye.

"That party I mentioned tonight? It was a masquerade gala."

Poppy stiffened. "Is that right?"

"The people I ran into? Mikhail and his driver."

As though his name were a spell in itself, the witch's expression shuttered. "I hadn't heard he was in town."

At least we weren't kicking things off with her denying she'd heard of the man, but she was lying. An infuriating waste of time.

"He's catching up with old friends, this time gathering the local covens—and killing them when he feels like it. We stopped by Rune the Day last night to offer our condolences for their lost members only to discover they must not have cared too much about their coven-mates. Instead of giving us the information we needed, they ratted us out to Mikhail. What about you? What have you heard?"

"You assume—"

There was the denial I'd expected.

"Cut the crap, Poppy. You know all there is to know about magical goings on in this city. Start lying to me now and things will not go well for you. Especially considering he left this for me as a souvenir."

I pulled the broken vial out of my thigh pocket and showed her the label at the bottom. "P.L. Coincidence?"

The blood drained from her face, but she threw her hands up to fend me off. "Oh hell no. You will not get me for associating with that man. I know better than that."

"You're telling me you're not selling illegal potions on the side?"

She dropped back in her chair with a huff. "Fine. You got me. The shop's doing well, but it only just covers rent. I may have a little side hustle going on. Nothing you need to get all... *you* about."

"This potion burned the crap out of my skin when it landed."

"Superficial wounds at most," she said. "If it did anything more than that, it's been altered by someone else. You can't fault a girl for offering self-defence potions in this city."

I tapped the vial against the arm of my chair. "You're telling me if I check your entire secret stock, I won't find anything maiming among them?"

She crossed her arms. "You won't. Selling that crap would only invite trouble into my store."

"You're already wrangling with a death dealer. How much more trouble can you invite?"

"Nuh-uh. He knows he's not welcome here. But I sell a few hundred potions a month. Those witches over at Rune the Day come here sometimes when they're too lazy to make their own."

"Why are all these witches looking to arm themselves?" Barrett asked, earning himself an incredulous stare from Poppy.

"Are you new to this world?" she asked. "The witches are pitted against the vampires, the vampires against the shifters, the shifters against the creatures, and the creatures come full circle and hunt us. The Hunter's Guild, the witch hunters, and the vampire hunters are all fumbling over themselves, too busy in their little circle jerk to actually take care of the problems. When they do stop comparing dick sizes long enough to take notice, it's usually to put down someone who's pissed them off, not the people actually causing the issue."

Hearing her perspective, my conscience nagged at me over the fact that I'd become too hands off. Things shouldn't be that bad. Not with so many groups supposedly tasked with overseeing them.

Retired or not, I would have to do better. At the very least check in with the hunters more often. They'd hate it, but if that's what it took to keep our worlds balanced, so be it.

"So you've heard enough to make you want to avoid him," I said. "Tell me."

Poppy stared me down for another beat, but she had to know I wouldn't back off.

A moment later, she lowered her gaze and said, "Fine. I might have picked up some info here and there. Folks coming in to buy supplies, topping up their herbs and other necessaries. They don't tell me what they're working on, but you're in this business long enough, you start to notice trends.

The sort of stuff they're walking out with? Makes my skin crawl. Nothing nasty on its own, but the idea of some of it being combined? Not good."

Barrett's eyes narrowed, and I tried to shrug off the creeping sense of dread that twisted my guts. I understood why Poppy had done nothing with her suspicions, even if I didn't like it. She was running a business and had no proof the goods bought would be used for anything horrible—or so she said. It wasn't like she could refuse to sell with nothing to back her up.

Still.

"What about the witches buying these supplies? Anything noteworthy about them?"

She raised a shoulder in a slow shrug. "Not really? Most of them are repeat customers, a few new faces. They don't tell me much."

"And what they do tell you?"

The teeth-pulling of this conversation was getting old, and I was about ready to remind her of the deal we'd made. The thin ice she walked on was cracking.

Another moment passed before Poppy launched herself out of her chair to pace the room.

"All right. Whatever. You want to know everything? There's a reason Mikhail is banned from my shop. The guy brought my coven into his inner circle about six months ago. About three months ago, I got out. I didn't like the web he was spinning. Too much trying to butter us up, not enough specifics about where he saw us going. It screamed double-cross." She shook her head. "None of my coven believed me. They didn't see the red flags, and now they're in so deep, they wouldn't be able to get out if they did. You talked about dead witches. They're probably not the first. Definitely not the last."

I frowned and rubbed the fingertips of my left hand together. "Poppy…"

"I know, I know, necromancy was supposed to be out. We made a deal, you can kill me for breaking it, blah, blah, blah. But I've never killed anyone. The only blood I've ever shed has been my own, and I've never summoned a ghoul or a demon, so that's gotta give me some brownie points, right?"

Frustration bubbled in my veins that she'd gotten involved at all, and I did my best to tamp it down. Priorities.

"Maybe. If you tell us where to find Mikhail. His driver hit the gas the second his butt touched the seat."

"I have no idea."

Quick response, roving gaze. "Lying."

Poppy snarled. "I hate when you do that. Look, if I spill the beans to you, I put my customers at risk. It slips out I sent you after them? There goes my reputation, and my *business* is at risk."

"You don't tell me, your business is at risk of not having an owner. Your choice."

I sensed Barrett's eyes on me and ignored him. If I wanted to threaten this woman, that was my prerogative. Based on our deal, her life was in my hands, which meant it was mine to threaten.

Poppy closed her eyes, let out a deep breath, and when she opened them again, the weight of her frustration—or her loathing—settled on my face. "I've heard they have secret meetings. One of my old coven members let it slip. Probably get her killed for telling you, but if it's a choice between her or me, I know where my loyalties lie."

I crossed my arms. "Good choice. Where do these meetings happen?"

"A warehouse outside the city. Near Mississauga."

"Who goes to these meetings? Just your old coven?"

If that's all it was, I was tempted to give it a miss. I didn't need more sad fools wasting my time and making promises they had no intention of keeping.

"When I was part of it, sure, but now I hear that's where most of them meet. He picks and chooses the strongest witches from each coven and keeps the rest on the sidelines as backup, but every week he's drawing more into that inner circle. Don't ask me why. I don't know, and I don't wanna know, but it can't be for any good reason."

"When is the next meet?"

Her expression turned fierce. "Why not kill me yourself if you want me dead so bad? These are not the kind of people I want to cross. Unlike you, they don't make deals."

"They also won't protect you if things go sour."

She snorted. "And you will?"

"I appreciate my allies."

Another stare-down until she finally let out a heavy breath. "It's been a while since their last meet, so I'd guess soon."

I watched her closely, taking in the faint tightening around her eyes and mouth, the way she curled her nails into her palms. She was keeping something back.

"Do you have a way of finding out?" I pinned her with a stare, making it clear what would happen if she pushed me.

She worked her jaw, then nodded. "Whatever. I'll put some feelers out and text you if I learn anything."

It wasn't what I wanted to hear, but it would have to do. If Poppy had lied about going to those meetings, she would already know the date but wouldn't want to give herself away. If she hadn't, I understood the position I was putting her in by forcing her hand. I also knew we would be giving ourselves away if word spread that we were asking around, but we had to take the risk.

Hopefully we would move faster than Mikhail.

Katerina

Lᴛʜᴏᴜɢʜ ɪᴛ ᴡᴀs clear Poppy would have preferred we leave her alone until she contacted us, I remained stubbornly in my seat. I refused to walk out of here without mining for every last detail of what we might expect if we attempted another raid. One coven had been simple enough, but if we were closing in on a larger group, Mikhail included, then we needed more information than when and where.

"How many people are typically at these meetings?"

Poppy propped her hands on her hips. "You're testing me, trying to get me to admit I go to them. I don't, so I don't know. If I'm right about the people coming in to buy supplies, then that's at least three local covens."

"So at minimum eighteen witches," I said for Barrett's benefit. By the way he pinched his lips together, I guessed he'd already done the math.

"And that's just the people buying from me," Poppy said. "I'm not the only occult shop in the neighbourhood, even if I am the best."

Her modesty was one of her nicer traits.

"I think it's best we prepare for at least twenty-four, then." I pursed my lips and tapped my fingers on the armrest.

Two dozen witches against an out-of-steam sorceress and a non-magical human. If the witches were the same calibre as the ones we'd encountered at Rune the Day, it would be doable. Maybe not as clean as how it had gone down last night, but doable. More than one Mikhail-level witch? We'd be getting into challenge territory.

"What sort of defences do they have?" I asked, and before Poppy could throw the same arguments at me, I held up a hand to fend her off. "Based on what you've sold them and what you know of these groups. It doesn't need to be accurate, just throw us the worst-case scenarios."

She dropped into her chair, crossed her legs, and sank into the cushions. "Basic spells for the most part. Some powders—the standards, itching, burning, numbing—some summoning spells. A few of them practice teaming up to cast spell circles, so if they have enough time there might be some anchored elemental magic lying around. The odd spirit."

My eye twitched, and I pressed my lips together. Poppy spoke as if it were nothing that people summoned entities onto this plane. Did she have any idea of the consequences of such stupidity?

Oh, but we can bind them.

Fools.

No spirit or demon could be fully bound. If they acted like they were, it was because they knew doing so would help them get what they wanted.

"Again, don't look at me like that, Kat. Demons aren't my jam. And I don't sell anything that would help them do it. I don't even sell chalk, specifically because of people like them. No one should encourage that crap."

If she was telling the truth, then at least on that we agreed. Not that Poppy was against summoning other things, as I knew well, but right now, the occasional corpse was a lesser evil compared to whatever else might be on the menu.

The real issue was that, after hearing the odds stacked against us, I didn't feel confident about walking into this confrontation. I could leave

Barrett outside and take the hits without worrying about dying, but that wasn't the way to get to Mikhail.

We'd tried low-key direct—maybe now it was time to go big.

Swallowing my pride at the thought of arming myself with witchcraft, I reached into the slim pocket along the waistband of my leather pants and pulled out the platinum credit card. In a smooth move, I tossed it to Poppy. "Everything you think they'll have on hand, I want something to counter it."

A slow smile spread across her face and grew into a wide grin. "Oh, this'll be fun."

With the light on, Poppy's shop was a different place from the gauntlet we'd walked on our arrival. The pot lights warmed the space and brightened the dark corners. Even the cat skulls looked less ominous than they had in the shadows.

Barrett stuck close to me, as determined not to touch anything now as he had been before. As though being in the presence of all these magical props risked tainting his purity. I wanted to shove him into the display case of crystals and tarot cards to see if he burst into flames.

Poppy moved behind the counter, pulled open a deep drawer, and began setting coloured glass vials on the surface. "All right. Two of each? Once you choose, I'll amp them up for you to do more damage. And no, I don't offer that service to my customers."

"One," Barrett said, staring at the counter with disdain. "My weapons will serve me better than any magic potion."

"Oh yeah, cowboy?" Poppy asked, raising one of her supremely well-maintained eyebrows. "Think you can run in shooting and get them before they get you? Think your little mundane guns will hold out in a room full of magic without backfiring?" She looked to me and jutted her thumb towards him as though to say, "Get a load of this guy."

I bit down on a smile. "Two of each. Amped up." When Barrett opened his mouth, I cut him off. "I'll carry all of them, I don't care, but I'd rather have them than not."

Whatever we found at this meeting, I wanted to be prepared. If everything went well, Mikhail wouldn't walk out of that warehouse, but the witches with him might not know what they'd gotten themselves into. I didn't want to use my power and burn them along with him if I could avoid it.

I'd never hear the end of it from Adrian, Barrett, Maera, or Rhys. Who needed that headache?

"Excellent." Poppy rubbed her hands together, and for the next fifteen minutes, she threw everything except the kitchen sink at me, including a satchel to carry it all in. "These people won't know what hit them."

"You'd better hope not," I said as I stuffed the vials into the satchel. "Believe me. Knowing Mikhail, you won't want to see what the world looks like if he gets what he wants."

By the time we left, which wasn't long before the shop opened for the day, Poppy had rung up my card for more than I'd ever spent on a bunch of witches' tools. I didn't feel any better about it than Barrett did, but at least I felt more certain I could hold my own in a fight.

Armed, tired, and ready for a nap before we started the next phase of our plan, Barrett and I headed back to the house.

"Do you trust her?" he asked.

"Not really. More than I do some people, though. I hold her leash, so it's in her best interests to work with me."

"That doesn't guarantee she will."

"I know very well how often people choose temptation over long-term survival. Yet my hope springs eternal that next time they'll prove themselves more intelligent than they have in the past."

He grunted as he pulled into the driveway, and I guessed that was the end of the conversation. Fine by me. I had a lot to think about, a lot to prepare for, and a lot of scenarios to plan out.

I got out of the car first and let us into the three-storey townhouse.

Adrian had bought it new and made it his own in the short time he'd lived here. It wasn't far from where Maera, Rhys, and I had lived, and I was glad Adrian had decided to hang on to it. I preferred it to forking out cash for a downtown hotel, and it came with the added benefit of happy memories to soak in after a thoroughly crappy night.

Bright maple flooring greeted me as I climbed the stairs to the main floor, where the living room-dining room awaited us in the front and the kitchen hid away in the back.

I gave my stomach a passing thought as I reached the stairs, but when it didn't grumble at me, I opted to skip the bedtime snack and head straight for my room on the second floor. It was the room I always stayed in, the nicest aside from the master bedroom on the third floor. An ensuite bathroom and three windows overlooked the front of the house, providing more natural light than any vampire would want.

Which, of course, was why Adrian had blacked out the windows on the top floor.

I planned to strip down to nothing and crawl into bed, fully intending to enjoy a few blessed hours of sleep while my subconscious worked through whatever we might face tomorrow. But when I turned to close the door, I found Barrett right behind me.

"What are you doing?" I asked, barring him from crossing the threshold into my safe space.

"I agree the living room would have been more comfortable, but you bypassed it." He spoke with such a lack of expression I squinted to see if I could make out the wires controlling him. He frowned. "We need to talk about what happened tonight."

I clenched my fists. "Which part?"

If he was about to blast me for threatening Poppy after I'd warned him I was going to do exactly that, I would be on the phone with Adrian so damned quick Barrett's ears would not so much burn as catch fire. Then I would put him on the first plane back home.

"You mean to tell me your actual plan of attack is to arm yourself to the teeth with magical potions and storm a coven meeting? *That* is you thinking with centuries of strategic experience?"

Oh, that part.

I rolled my shoulders to relieve the tension I'd recently named Barrett. "I know you have years of training to back you up, but as much as you struggle to believe it, this is not my first hunt. When you're out of options, sometimes you have to throw everything you've got at the threat and trample it beneath you. I'll give the witches a chance to get out first, but if we know this is where Mikhail will be, then yes, I'll put strength over finesse. Wouldn't you?"

He blinked. Slowly. Judgement oozed off him as though it were a physical slime, and my hackles rose.

"You've already said you don't trust the witch," he said. "You don't think she's running to her coven right this second and telling them about our visit? If she doesn't plan to be at that meeting herself, she's got friends who are, and she won't want them getting hurt. They'll know we're coming."

"Of course they will."

He started, no doubt shocked that I would deign to agree with him.

Despite what he thought of me, I was capable of reason and logic.

"Mikhail will expect us around every corner. We've lost the element of surprise. Which is all the more reason to go on the offensive. Whatever it takes to set him off balance. At the same time, Poppy's not stupid. She knows we'll be going in to make Mikhail bleed, so it's more likely she'll tell her buddies not to show up if they want to keep breathing."

Barrett shook his head. "So you really do plan to, once again, waltz in and start throwing magic until we reach Mikhail?"

I leaned my shoulder against the door jamb. "No, that's only if things go wrong. I plan to waltz in, spot Mikhail, and burn his heart out of his chest. His followers can scream and wail and tear out their hair as much as they like, but the threat will be neutralized."

He blinked again, and I was starting to hear the curse words associated with the gesture. Very diplomatic of him to utter them so silently.

"You can't seriously think it'll be that easy," he said, and again, all I could hear was the echo of my nagging inner voice telling me I was incapable of pulling this off.

My self-restraint snapped. "No, I don't. I think it's going to be a huge pain in my ass and everything is going to go wrong, like the rest of this hunt. Especially the part about you being here with me, dogging my steps and insisting you have a say in everything."

His nostrils flared. "You couldn't even stop him on a quiet street before he got into his car."

Red crept around my vision, and I struggled to breathe through it. "If I hadn't needed to save you from some serious magic burn, I would have. You got in my way. Stay out of it next time, and we won't have a problem. You are my backup, not my partner. I don't care what Adrian says or how you feel about it. I've got over eight hundred years on you, so if either of us is leading this show, it's me."

The lines around his eyes hardened. "Adrian has over a thousand years on you, but somehow he's managed to avoid your up-his-own-ass attitude."

I ruffled under the observation. "He hasn't, he's just been around long enough to learn how to hide it better. Believe me, if he were in my shoes, he would be patting you on the head and telling you to mind your place in the nicest possible way. If he didn't enthrall you and force you to do his will. Remember who you're dealing with, Barrett. I'm not some witch with potions and spells." Never mind the satchel at my hip arguing to the contrary. I swallowed my shame that it was necessary. "Adrian is not some nice benefactor with a blood kink. We're immortal. We're magical. We're more powerful than you can imagine. All right? So yes, I believe you know what you're talking about when it comes to manoeuvring a room, and yes, I believe you can wield your mundane weapons with very impressive skill, but we aren't in your world right now. We're in mine."

I stopped to catch my breath, and for a moment we stared at each other, possibly both taken aback by my unexpected tirade.

How much of it did I even mean, and how much was a result of how pissed off I was by the men in my life? Barrett judging me, Mikhail looking down on me, Emrick ignoring my simple requests. Even Adrian had foisted Barrett on me when he knew I disliked the guy.

But the reasons for my rant didn't matter. It was out there now, and damn if I was going to step backwards to undo any of the damage I might have caused to our turbulent relationship.

Because yes, I did intend to come up with a better plan than "burst through doors—magic blast." That was a great way to burn down buildings and get the wrong people killed. But I was in no mood to sit down for a cozy brainstorming session.

Barrett might think I was full of myself, but who was he to talk as if he thought he understood our situation better than I did? He hadn't seen half the shit I had in my years hunting the dark and depraved, and he best pray to whatever god he believed in he never did.

But fuck, Adrian was going to tear me a new one when he heard about this.

"Fine," Barrett said at last. "You take the lead, and I'll shut up and follow. But know that if I see things going sideways, I'll step in. I've already told you—"

I pushed away from the door jamb and waved my hand in the air. "Yeah, yeah, you won't let my arrogance or anticlimactic skills get in the way of stopping Mikhail. Believe me, Barrett, you have no idea how much I want that man dead. There is very little, barring my own improbable death, that could stop me."

He looked as though he were about to say something else, but he didn't have a chance before my phone buzzed.

I pulled it out of my pocket and swiped up to open Poppy's text. First came an address, followed by a message.

This just in—that meet? 2nite. 9pm. Good luck.

19

Katerina

Poppy's text shoved a wrench into my whole "crawling into bed" plans. Also my whole "leave Barrett out of the loop until I had everything sorted" plans.

Now, instead of being curled up under my blankets obsessively running through scenarios of all the ways Mikhail might get the upper hand on me—and what his end goal might be—I was in the kitchen *talking* about all the ways Mikhail might get the upper hand on me.

With Barrett.

Who was enjoying the discussion of my possible failures more than I'd seen him enjoy anything in the ten years I'd known him. I think he almost cracked a smile at one point.

The worst part was his input had been helpful, and I patted myself on the back for being able to acknowledge it. While experience had taught me a lot, I had to admit there was a cap on how far it would get me. I'd been involved in almost every type of raid—both as raider and raidee—but my still-very human memory only retained so much. Barrett's more recent training served to fill in the gaps, and as the sun rose high enough to spill through the kitchen windows, we had the foundations of a pretty solid plan.

"It will only work if your buddy pitches in," I said, frowning at the sketch Barrett had drawn of the warehouse.

The address Poppy had sent, a small warehouse tucked well off a Mississauga highway, was about an hour away. The photos online didn't show much in the way of security, but these were dark witches we were talking about. They wouldn't leave their defences down if they'd planned an intense ritual that would require time and concentration.

"Tony says they'll have no problem hacking into the cameras and shutting them down."

"And the magical element?" I asked. "I can make out three entrances. The front doors here, the loading bay here on the side, and then this secondary entrance up here on the fire escape. That's a lot of ground for the two of us to cover to clear it."

"He says he'll get back to us on that."

A phone on the table buzzed.

If that was the witch hunter already, I'd be impressed by his timing. But when the phone buzzed again, I realized it was mine ringing, not Barrett's.

I picked it up to see Rhys's face smiling at me. Dread speared through my stomach, and I rushed to answer. "Is everything all right?"

"Maybe?" His voice was shaky. I wished he were here so I could put my arms around him.

"Deep breaths. Start with a few deep breaths, all right?"

He did as I said, and after the third one, it didn't sound nearly as rough.

"All right, can you tell me what's going on? Is everyone okay at home?"

Worry shredded my insides that something had happened to Maera and only lessened its hold slightly when Rhys said, "We're fine. I had a dream. Except I don't think it was a dream, you know?"

"You had another vision?"

Barrett stared at me, a pen already in his hand as he pulled a blank sheet of paper towards him. I put the phone on speaker and set it in the middle of the table.

"I saw colours," Rhys said. "Bright, vivid colours. Flying in arcs and wrapping in circles in the air. It was really cool… except people were screaming. Running. Trying to get away. Faces weren't clear, but everyone seemed really frustrated."

Barrett glared at the satchel filled with potions sitting on the empty chair at the table, having already made the connection between flying colours and magic. He wasn't wrong that they were dangerous, but I wasn't about to leave them at home.

"Anything else?" I asked.

"No." Rhys sounded so defeated, I felt bad for asking, but I reminded myself he would never get stronger unless he practiced holding on to as many details as possible. Questions would help him, even if they pained me.

"It's okay," I said. "You remembered enough to call me. That's a huge leap forward. What about impressions? Any sense of how big the group is? Or what sort of magic they're throwing around?"

"The colours were coming from both sides. All directions. Everything was a huge mishmash."

Didn't that bode well for us.

It was fine. I'd already known we were likely walking into a trap. If we had to give up stealth, we'd find another way to take them by surprise.

My magic bubbled in my blood, longing to come to the surface, but I tamped it down, not wanting to destroy Adrian's lovely blue-hued kitchen.

"Thanks for this, Rhys. Go back to sleep. Call again if you See anything else."

"Will do," he said glumly. "Good luck."

I hung up, and Barrett pulled his sketch of the warehouse towards him.

"How accurate are his visions usually?" he asked.

I shrugged. "Accurate enough. What we haven't figured out is how definitive they are. Is he Seeing things as they'll play out now? As they'll be if we change our plans? Depending on the vision, I prefer to see them as general expectations rather than specific outcomes."

Barrett grunted, and I suspected he would prefer them not to factor in at all.

"That being said," I continued, "if everything is about to devolve into chaos, that pushes me to say we should skip being sneaky and make use of the front doors. Or even the loading bay. At least then we have a giant exit at our backs. Whether Rhys's visions are flexible or not, I think it's safe to say our night isn't going to go smoothly."

I chewed on the side of my thumb. "I knew I should have gone in alone last night. At least then you could have been the unknown. But now you're right—they'll be expecting both of us."

Another buzzing phone.

"Tony," Barrett said.

The witch hunter had come through.

"He says he can have half a dozen hunters waiting for us at the warehouse by the time we get there."

I released a breath and allowed a weight to go with it. Six trained hunters, one Barrett, and one me against a few dozen coven witches? Yeah, that much we could handle.

"Tell Tony I'll owe him one. And I don't dole out favours loosely. All right." I slapped my hands down on the table and rose to my wobbly feet. "Now I can sleep."

Thirteen hours later, well past the February sundown, we got out of the car down the street from the warehouse. My hands trembled at my sides with anticipation. The magical strength coming from the building was potent even from two blocks away, and my hopes surged that this time Mikhail would be standing with his followers.

Barrett's hand rested on the grip of his gun where it sat holstered at his waist, and the handle of his knife glinted on the other side. Stubborn to the last, he'd refused any of the vials Poppy had sold us.

From the street, the warehouse appeared dark and no sounds reached us, but as we got closer, the pulsing of a magical ward made my fingertips itch. Barrett made to cross it, but I grabbed his arm and pulled him back. His first instinct was to try to snatch his arm away, but he must have realized I wasn't playing around, because he backed up. I rested my hand against the air to get a feel for the spell. Strong. Layered. Many witches working together to cloak whatever they were doing behind it.

"They've warded themselves," I whispered.

"Will they know if we cross it?"

I shook my head. "Some sorcerers used to be able to create wards that were bound to them like that, but this is witchcraft. It's just a spell. That's not to say it won't trigger some kind of alarm, though. Give me a second to see if I can find the source."

"I'll text Tony. Give him the heads up."

So far there had been no sign of the hunters, but I agreed with Barrett. The last thing we needed was for a bunch of cocky witch hunters to stumble over the ward and give us away before we were in position.

With my eyes closed, I pushed deeper into the spell, following the magic to see if it was tied to anything beyond the cloaking spell. At first I sensed nothing, but buried deep within, like a tiny flashing light, was a second weave of magic.

"Clever ducks."

I had to give them credit. These witches knew what they were doing.

Too bad for them, so did I.

The taste of the second spell led me to a nearby tree and a plastic owl perched on a leafless branch. It had been hidden by the shadows, so I never would have noticed it. If I interpreted the magic correctly, the owl would have screeched an alarm as soon as anyone passed through the ward.

"Think you can dismantle it?" I asked.

Barrett jumped for the lower branch of the tree and heaved himself onto it. He picked up the owl and flipped it over. "Simple device. Dollar store crap."

He tossed it down to me, and I saw the switch on the back. Huh.

"I guess these guys are advocates for the Work Smart Not Hard mentality." I made sure the owl was off and threw it to the ground under the tree. The surviving witches could collect it after I'd finished with them if they wanted to use it again.

Barrett swung back to the ground. "Any others we need to worry about?"

I checked the weave of magic again, but this time there was only the ward. "I think we're good. Keep your eyes open, though. If these people are of Poppy's ilk, we might need to watch out for falling axes."

As we crossed the ward, the appearance of the warehouse changed. Light glowed through the windows, and a hum of many voices carrying the same note reached us. A focusing chant. They were just starting their evening.

Warning bells screamed in my head, and for a moment, I couldn't move.

So far, everything had gone swimmingly, but the swimmingness in itself concerned me. Mikhail had to know I was coming for him, so where were the sentries? Were they all posted inside? A line of defence around whoever was performing the ritual? I wished we had eyes inside the warehouse, but Tony had texted Barrett saying there were no cameras for them to hack into. Another advantage gone.

"Where the hell are the hunters?" I asked, my nerves making me huffy.

Or maybe I would have been anyway. I hated having to rely on any third-party organization. If my magic were at its height, I wouldn't need them. I wouldn't need Barrett. Those witches could have thrown anything at me, and I'd have returned the volley tenfold.

Instead, I was left with showy, half-effective toys in a room where everyone bought from the same shop.

Maybe that was why Mikhail hadn't bothered with defences. He knew we were outmatched.

Barrett pulled out his phone as I stood fuming. "He says they're en route. Got detoured by an accident on the way in."

"Fuck." It felt so good to say that I repeated it another five times. Was this a case of raging bad luck, or were we looking at traitors within the hunters' ranks? Yet another question for me to dig into later. "We can't stand around waiting for them. Once these guys finish the focusing spell, they'll move on to whatever comes next. Either more witches are going to die in there, or Mikhail is going to get what he's really after. I don't want either of those things to happen."

Barrett pulled his shoulders back and looked towards the road as though hoping a van full of hunters would pull up. When no miracle happened, he turned to me. "What do you have in mind?"

"We make use of the fire escape entrance and rain hell down on them. Or we bust through the front doors and—"

"I get the idea."

He frowned at the warehouse, his dark eyes glazing over as he considered our options.

I summoned my magic into my hands and let the fire spill across my palms and up the backs of my gloves.

"I don't like it," he said.

I waited, picking up on the pending "but."

It never came, and in the silence, reason and my lizard brain poked at my impatience to grab Mikhail.

"You think we should leave," I said. "Try again later."

Barrett nodded. "Not ideal, but without backup, we'll be overpowered."

I wanted to ignore his logic. If we took a pass on this opportunity, we might not get another one. Even if Poppy had ratted us out, tonight was still our best—possibly last—shot before Mikhail carried out his plans. I could leave Barrett behind and run in myself, fight my way through the witches, and go after the blood witch. I wouldn't come out unscathed, but the odds were good I'd come out breathing.

Unless they were prepared for me to do exactly that. If they swarmed me and left me incapacitated, Mikhail would undoubtedly test my immortality more than I ever had. Maybe Emrick would show up in time to whisk me to safety, but was that really a risk I was willing to take?

I'd run after Mikhail at the gala, but that had been me against him. Not even I was foolish enough to attempt going up against three full covens.

I cursed again, fire licking my arms as I fought to get my power and my rage under control. "If I lose my chance of getting Mikhail because your buddy dropped the ball, I'm going to torch his house. Get updates on those hunters, and you'd better hope they have a better excuse than getting stuck in traffic. If anyone else dies, it's on their heads."

I stomped back towards the ward, leaving Barrett to catch up.

A flicker of light caught my eye. A spell circle, previously hidden where it had been drawn in the snow, glowed a bright red, and I just avoided stepping on it as the magic released. Barrett and I were thrown back by the force of the blast.

My breath burst from my lungs as I struck the ground, and I barely had time to recover before the doors to the warehouse opened and the witches spilled out.

20

Katerina

THE MOMENT MY back hit the snow, I used the momentum to flip onto my feet. Barrett was in a fighting stance beside me nearly as quickly, gun drawn.

I reversed my heat, easy to do on a cold night, and crouched to set my hands on the ground. Frost spilled from my fingers, thickening into ice that stretched towards the front doors.

As three witches ran out, vials in their hands, they slipped and fell hard on their brand-new skating rink. The tinkling of smashing glass was followed closely by screams as their potions splashed over their hands and faces.

From inside, the chant continued, though the voices were less in tune—or maybe it was simply that there were fewer witches adding their power to the ritual. No longer did it sound like a focusing spell. Whatever their purpose was tonight, they were going for it, party-crashers or no.

More witches rushed outside. The first two tripped over their coven-mates, not expecting them to be on the ground, and another one caught her footing only to lose it on the ice.

If I weren't trying to keep track of the vermin pouring from the ware-house, I would have been entertained by the performance.

Unfortunately, the witches kept coming.

Barrett fired off two shots, and two witches dropped to the ground, screaming and clutching their legs. He fired again, but a woman shouted a spell, and the bullet ricocheted away from her and pierced the head of a witch trying to get back to his feet.

Blood spilled across the snow, and I pressed forward. I didn't want these people to die. I hated killing people. Had once sworn off ever doing it again. But they kept putting themselves in a position to be killed, and I didn't have time to sit down and lecture them about their poor life decisions.

I grabbed two vials out of my satchel and flung them at random into the growing crowd at the door. The first one cracked on the ice and released a haze that caused one witch to bend at the waist heaving; the other smashed with an eardrum-bursting *pop* that brought another three to their knees.

For all the reasons I had not to trust Poppy, I had to give her credit for being creative. She'd warned me her potions were best used from a distance, and I crossed my fingers I reached Mikhail before I had to find out why.

Barrett raised his weapon to fire again, but a woman with spectacular aim launched a vial at him. The glass smashed against his hands, and smoke rose from his sizzling flesh. He dropped the gun into the snow, bared his teeth, and freed his knife, shifting his fighting posture so quickly and smoothly, I would have guessed he was magical himself.

Then I remembered who I was dealing with. As Adrian's human thrall, Barrett reaped the benefits of the blood exchange. Heightened reflexes, senses, healing. The man might hate magic, but it was likely to save his life tonight.

The witch who'd thrown the vial sneered and readied another one, but Barrett launched himself into the crowd at the door, tackling her inside.

I cursed his name and followed. We'd been doing well keeping their numbers blocked off in the doorway, but it seemed Rhys's premonition was about to come true.

My heart raced with anticipation of the greater fight, of getting that much closer to Mikhail. The air tingled with magic that made the hair on my arms dance, sullied by the underlying stench of smoke, sweat, and dark power.

Vials in hand, I stepped over the moaning, groaning witches on the ground. One of them grabbed for me, but I kicked out my leg and caught them in the head, sending them sliding farther across the ice.

The moment I crossed the threshold, more magic hummed around me from the three witches guarding the door. Vaguely, I took in what we were dealing with—those fighting and the six still sitting on the floor chanting. There were far more than the number we'd anticipated, likely by another dozen. I focused more closely on the three in front of me and the vials they held at their sides.

They threw in tandem, and I dropped mine to the ground, grateful when the glass didn't shatter, as I summoned a fireball between my hands and hurled it at them. The flames devoured whatever magic they'd tried to send my way but petered out before it reached them. The smoke reeked of charred power, an acidic tang that burned the back of my nose and tickled my gag reflex.

Not giving them time to recover, I picked up the vials I'd dropped and threw them at the witches' feet. Enchanted green flames caught their pants, and the three scattered as they tried to put the fire out. Like the smoke, the enchanted fire stank, adding a whiff of sulphur to the already nauseating aroma.

One man, screaming and slapping at his clothes, stumbled into a stack of shipping crates, and the fire spread, quickly consuming the far left side of the building and blocking off the loading bay. One exit gone. Smoke wafted to fill the rest of the room, but still the witches sitting in the centre continued their chant.

Through the haze, I spotted Barrett. In the few minutes my attention had been elsewhere, he'd managed to wrangle four witches and had them face-down on the ground with their hands zip-tied behind them. Blood seeped down the side of his face, and his hand was covered in blisters, but none of his injuries appeared to have slowed him down.

Trusting him to take care of himself, I focused on the half-dozen people within the ritual circle.

"Mikhail!" I shouted over their voices, directing my call to the person sitting at the top of the room. He wore a hood pulled low over his face, but at his name, he tilted his head as though considering me from the shadows.

At least, I thought it was him. A faint floral scent I recognized from the masquerade drifted beneath the sweat and smoke, but it wasn't followed by the hit of spicy cologne. I couldn't see his face, and from where I stood his shoulders looked narrower than they had in his costume, more hunched. But the way they sat, clearly leading the circle, the power flowing off them—who else could it be?

I made my way forward and threw more vials as two witches tried to stop me. The splash of potion as the glass shattered coated my legs, and my leather pants smoked. Poppy had been right—farther was better. This close, I'd have to draw on my own power if I wanted to win.

Hands at my sides, I summoned fire into my palms. Three chanting witches at the back of the circle rose to stand against me, their low, monotone voices lending an air of eeriness to their already creepy appearance. Their eyes flashed purple, filled with power they must have gathered during their focusing spell.

Were all the witches in this circle sharing power? If so, our position had grown more precarious. So far, we'd dominated this fight because our resources were matched. But two against a group of fully fueled witches?

Before I could process the hit to my confidence, a loud cry drew my attention to the left. I turned in time to watch Barrett fall to one knee with his hand clasped to his face. Blood spilled between his fingers, and I followed the source of his pain to a young man holding what appeared to be a bag of pop rocks. Only they weren't candy. They were mini-explosives enchanted to detonate with the right incantation and very much banned by the witch hunters. Unless Poppy was selling more than weaponized potions—and I intended to find out—someone else in this city had been very, very naughty.

More fire warmed my palm, and I launched it at the witch's hand. The bag of explosives started to snap, and his eyes flew wide as he realized what was about to go off in his palm. Except the idiot didn't just drop the bag. He threw it as far as he could into the mass of crates against the opposite side of the building from where the fire already raged. The explosives went off, and smoke filled the corner as the crates were consumed.

My lungs grew scratchy, and I stifled my cough, knowing once I started I would struggle to stop. We had to get out of here.

I turned to check on Barrett, but as I angled my face away from the room, a spell struck the back of my neck, sending sharp pangs of electricity through my body. I bit down on a scream and whirled on my heel, ready to launch an assault of my own.

"I really don't want to kill you." I doubted my declaration, ragged as it was with the influx of smoke in my lungs, would have any effect but felt it needed to be said.

A few witches showed some level of sense. Not many, but I spotted two slipping away and tearing out of the warehouse. Though whether they were running from me or from the fire creeping along the wall and devouring the pallets closer to the middle of the room, I didn't know. Didn't really matter.

We were now down to ten, and my waning confidence was returning. I'd given the rest of them an out. If they didn't choose to take me up on it…

I threw a fireball at the three witches in front of me, and they scattered as they ran.

In the space they left, I reversed my heat and set my hands on the ground. Already, despite my measured use, my magic was circling the drain, frayed and lethargic as it travelled across the floor and crept over the witches still chanting.

Standing so close to them, I felt the surge in the air of their magic pooling together. It prickled my skin and made my teeth buzz. But the layers of frost spreading over their laps caused more than one to stumble over their incantation. Their magic hitched.

The person at the top of the circle stiffened and rose to their feet. I opened my mouth to shout once more to Mikhail, to challenge him in front of the others and force his followers to see how worthless their loyalty was.

The words dried on my tongue.

It wasn't him.

Whoever was leading this circle was smaller and seemed strangely bent at the waist.

The chanting finally stopped, the remaining witches pulled from their spell, and their leader hobbled away—older, maybe, or injured. I chased after them. If they were at the head of the circle, they had to know where Mikhail was or what his plans were.

But I'd barely closed the distance between us when the three witches I'd blasted with my fire were in my face again. As one, they shouted a spell, and a glowing red circle formed in the air, growing brighter until it burst, and fire exploded in a searing heat that threw me to the ground in a heap of singed hair and screaming nerve endings.

My throat ached as I held back my cries. The pain was excruciating, but if they thought this was the first time I'd been almost burned alive, they were about to be disappointed.

Rage filled me, and frustration—just as Rhys had Seen—drove me back to my feet. I pulled the dregs of my magic into my palms and readied myself to throw it at them.

Barrett stepped in front of me.

At the last second, I was able to redirect the fire into another stack of shipping crates on the other side of the room, and my eardrums pulsed with the burst of three more gunshots.

New screams filled my head, leaving me wrapped in a world of confusion and pain. My power was exhausted, my burns had already begun to heal—a torture in itself—and Mikhail was nowhere to be found.

Seemingly hadn't been here at all. Again.

Someone grabbed my arm, and I lurched away, then heaved a breath on finding Barrett beside me.

"Let's go," he wheezed between heavy coughs. He removed his hand from his face to reveal a series of gaping wounds across his cheek that made me flinch.

All around us, the witches fled. The smoke was so thick, I couldn't make out the back wall and the chalk circle on the floor was nothing more than a collection of blurred lines.

My head swam, and I gave up the fight against the coughs that wracked my body.

Barrett wrapped his arms around me, but he was stumbling too, both of us on the brink of collapse.

My vision darkened along the edges as my lungs clogged with smoke. Not a moment too soon, fresh, cold air reached us from outside. It was enough to renew my strength for a moment, and I heaved Barrett and I out of the warehouse into the snow. The skating rink I'd made caught us, and we skidded across the surface, clearing a few metres in seconds.

Which saved us.

As soon as we hit the end of the ice, something inside the warehouse burst. The upper windows exploded outwards as the fire roared into the dark night and devoured what was left of the building.

21

Katerina

S HAKING WITH FURY and adrenaline, I dropped into the passenger seat of Barrett's SUV.

He slammed the door on the driver's side, the only sign that he was anything other than calm.

We sat there for a full minute, both of us staring out the windshield into the shadows created by the rising fire.

That had not gone well. I didn't need Barrett's insightful comments to know it. This time, however, it hadn't been my poor planning. I'd been good. Responsible. Sure, I'd missed the spell circle, but it had been well hidden under the snow. Too well hidden, frankly. None of the witches in that warehouse had shown the kind of power required to cast a spell that strong.

My thoughts drifted to the hooded person leading their ritual. Had they been the one to leave the trap?

Pain shot into my skull, and I relaxed my jaw before I cracked a tooth. Mikhail wasn't working alone, a detail neither Raisa nor Poppy had shared with me.

"Take us back to Poppy's," I ordered.

Barrett didn't take his eyes off the road as he started the car and pulled into the lane.

We didn't speak on the trip, though I was certain we were both buzzing with questions. By the time we reached Moon in Venus, one question in particular dominated my mind.

"After I'm done with her, we're going to have a chat with Tony. I want to know why the hunters fucked off when we needed them. If they have a rat among them, they need to crush it."

"Agreed."

I finally turned to look at him, taking in the deep gashes along his cheek. The bleeding had stopped, but the wounds looked nasty.

"Maybe Poppy can help you clean that up. Some free healing potions are the least she can do."

His expression darkened. "It's fine. It'll heal on its own."

"Is that experience talking or your stubbornness?" I asked. "Because I'm not in the mood to let your prejudices slow us down if your injuries get infected. You accuse me of being rash? I won't deny it. But your hatred of magic is getting in our way as much as my hatred of planning."

We glowered at each other. I wasn't backing down on this. Tonight we'd had a taste of what we truly faced, and as it stood, we weren't enough. And that had been without Mikhail among them. If he'd been there, we might not have escaped the warehouse before it blew.

The realization restarted the tremors that had finally subsided in my hands, and I channelled my nerves into anger. Someone was going to pay for shattering the blinders I'd comfortably worn for the past few decades.

"Fine," Barrett said after a millennium had passed.

I blinked, my brain needing a chance to catch up on what he was agreeing to. Right. The healing potions. I nodded in approval.

"Let's go find out what this witch held back from us," I said.

Once he stopped the car, I got out, slammed the door behind me, and marched to the private door behind its curtain of ivy.

"Are you sure you don't want to calm down before you go in there?" Barrett asked.

I whipped around to face him and found his gaze focused on the flames dancing over my fingertips. "No, I don't want to *calm down*," I snapped, but I shook out my hands to clear the magic. "I killed people tonight, Barrett. I hate killing people. If Poppy set me up, then she might very well be next."

Without giving him a chance to offer any further argument, I reversed my heat and set my hand on the door. The handle froze, and I snapped it off and jerked the door open.

As soon as I crossed the threshold, I shouted, "Proserpine!" into the silent stairwell. At first, no sound of movement reached me from above, but when I added a firm, "If you want to have a shop in the morning, you'll get down here this instant," there came the satisfying scurry of feet and a creak of floorboards. The door opened at the top of the stairs, and a flustered Poppy wearing purple sweats and a grey tank top appeared in the doorway.

She looked surprised to find us here, but the shock quickly turned into worry at the sight of me fuming.

Barrett was probably right that I should have taken a moment to catch my breath, but I was too wired to breathe. I was too hyped up to do anything other than storm up the stairs, grab Poppy by the throat, and slam her into the wall. Her wide eyes gaped at me, and I sneered at her terror.

"Three years, Poppy. I gave you three years of extra life when I should have taken it the night you tried to raise that cemetery. I was lenient, and where did that get me? Sent into battle without all the facts. Mikhail wasn't there, someone else was, and now there are a handful of dead witches burning to ash who could have still been breathing tomorrow. What do you say? Did you know Mikhail wouldn't be there?"

"No—no, I swear," she rasped.

I tensed as a hand rested on my arm and turned to look at Barrett. He'd followed me up the stairs and was glaring at Poppy even as he tried to pull me back.

"She won't be able to talk if she passes out," he said, and his calm logic convinced me to loosen my hold.

Releasing Poppy, I stepped away. She sputtered and coughed as she rubbed her throat, and although I expected to see anger, none of it stared back at me as she gained her feet.

Instead, the depth of her remorse almost pushed me to sympathy.

"I'm sorry," she said. "I didn't know. I had no idea. I reached out to my friend like you asked, told her I'd changed my mind and was thinking about going to the meet. She got back to me with the address, but a few minutes later, she messaged me again, told me there was a rumour going around that someone planned to raid the warehouse and if anyone came to the shop asking about it, I should tell them—you—where to go. I thought it was a false trail, that the warehouse would be empty. I didn't think they'd try to kill you. What the fuck kind of thing are they involved in where they would commit murder to make it happen?"

The horror in her eyes at the realization of how far her friends had gone tempted me to believe her.

"How about we go upstairs, and you can tell us the rest of what you know?" I said. "Also, Barrett needs some healing on his face. Last thing this guy needs is more scars to scare people away."

She replied with a stunned nod and, on shaking legs, led the way into her apartment. The space was cozier tonight than it had been this morning, with lights on in the kitchen and living room and a pot of peppermint tea sitting on the table beside the armchair. Poppy didn't offer us any, but I didn't think she was in a state of mind to think of anyone other than her old associates.

Good. I wanted her to stew in the nightmare she might have been caught up in if she'd stuck around with Mikhail's group. I wanted her to be terrified at the idea of being a part of it. Maybe then she'd stay on the straight and narrow and I wouldn't have to kill her the next time I came to town.

"So," I said, resuming the seat I'd taken this morning while Barrett once again perched uncomfortably on the wooden dining chair.

As if we'd never left.

As if everything that had happened since this morning had been a time-out.

With no people dead by my hand.

My stomach twisted, but I forced my conscience aside and turned my attention to Poppy. "Mikhail. Why wasn't he there tonight, and who is he working with? He never struck me as the type to share the limelight."

She puttered around the kitchen, gathering various supplies that she spread out on the dining table in front of Barrett. "All I can tell you is what the gossips are saying. That he has some kind of patron. No one's ever seen them beyond a glimpse here or there. Enough to know they're old. And powerful. But they stick to the background."

Barrett and I watched as she mixed a green potion with a white powder to create a—somehow—bright blue paste.

"Mikhail's the one at the head of this thing, though, and he's planning something big," she continued. "I meant it when I said he never went into detail when I was there, but something in the way he talked about it—this wild glint in his eyes made me realize I didn't want to be within fifty metres of whatever it was."

Barrett narrowed his eyes but remained still as Poppy smeared the salve over his cheek. He hissed in a sharp breath at the contact, and I braced for him to attack the witch. When his expression went blank, I knew the pain had disappeared.

"I went to three meetings with my friends, and each one drew us in deeper," Poppy said. "He started out his meetings like any regular coven leader might, going on about magic and exploring our power, brushing off the dust that prevented our true strength from shining. But with each meeting, it got a bit darker. Talking about absorbing power, taking down enemies. He started to sound like some video game villain. Or, you know, a cult leader."

I tried to imagine what those meetings might have seemed like to a fledgling witch and understood how so many of them had wound up fighting to the death for the chance to come out ahead.

People turned to spellcraft for three reasons: to help, to learn, or to gain power. The ones who wanted to help would never have sat through the first of Mikhail's meetings. In fact, his reputation would have been enough to keep them away. The third, though. They not only would have been drawn to him, but they would have drunk in his words and promises.

Poppy fell into the second camp. It was why I'd spared her life three years ago. She hadn't always made the best decisions, but her intent had never been to harm. She wanted to explore her power, find out how much she could do with it, and sometimes that meant making very serious, very stupid mistakes. But that shouldn't cost anyone their life.

As long as that continued to be the case, she would keep breathing.

"So you walked?"

"Yeah, I walked." Poppy wiped her hands on a cloth and sealed the rest of the salve in a plastic container. She'd changed her nail polish since this morning, and it was now a bright, bold blue that seemed wholly at odds with the nervous woman in front of me. "Took my life in my hands to leave, but I did it."

I frowned. "He threatened you?"

"As good as. He talked a big game about anyone being free to walk if they didn't want in on the ground floor, but when I ran for the door, I had to swear on my life to keep his secret."

She pressed her fingers into her eyes and released a frustrated scream. When she caught her breath, she pointed one of those blue-tipped claws in my face. "So you'd better protect me, kitty Kat, because if he finds out I told you any of this, I'll be as dead as those witches you killed tonight."

22

Emrick

I PACED THE length of the burned-out warehouse, feeling restless and stifled.

The scent of Kat's magic lingered in the air, and I imagined her being caught up in whatever battle had happened here tonight. I'd escorted six witches into the afterlife, but none of them had been overly chatty.

According to one of them, a mad woman had charged the building and set everyone on fire.

That sounded like my sorceress, but only if she'd had good reason.

I'd asked what they'd been doing here, and they'd all given the same answer. Mikhail had promised them power. More than they'd ever attain on their own. And they'd tasted it.

Some of them had even believed their deaths were worth it for that one fleeting moment of triumph.

I shoved my fingers through my hair and stopped at what had once been the front doors. Remainders of the icy patch Kat had created glinted in the obscured moonlight, and I found myself smiling as I imagined her watching the witches slide across it. She always did know how to take people by surprise.

Though not enough to win by the look of it.

Anger rippled through me, and I rolled my shoulders to release the tension building in my muscles.

My help wasn't wanted.

I'd been good about respecting her wishes for so many years, but recently I'd fought an almost daily longing to return to her side.

On an exhale, I summoned the mists and stepped into the afterlife. The barren landscape greeted me as it always did—a wide stretch of empty field with leafless trees reaching their arms into the murky sky. Shades of grey with no colour to break up the monochrome. Beautiful in its emptiness. Peaceful.

Here and there, glints of light wound through the dry grass and around the withered tree trunks, lost souls that had yet to make their way to the river. Waiting for direction. For clarity. Until then, listless.

I empathized with them.

When I stepped through the mist again, I stood in Adrian's library. The vampire was settled in his usual armchair, a glass of blood by his elbow, a book on his lap.

"Developments?" he asked without looking up.

"Not as much as I'd have liked." I crossed my arms and stared out the window over the snow-covered gardens.

"They'll find their answers," Adrian said. "You know Katerina won't let this lie, and Barrett will push her until they solve it."

I smirked. "So that's why you sent him with her."

Adrian shrugged, but I caught the faint quirk in the corner of his mouth. "I may have considered the possibility that their mutual dislike and shared stubbornness might be what it takes to bring Mikhail to his knees."

My smile dried up. "I could end this so much faster. With no one else needing to suffer for it."

At that, Adrian raised his head. "No one except for you, you mean. Or do you not matter?" When I didn't answer, he cocked his head. "If that weren't reason enough, you'd be daring Katerina's wrath—not only for your sacrifice but for stealing her victory. You'd be setting yourself back decades with her."

I huffed and shoved my hands in my pockets. "She should have been able to turn every one of those witches to cinders without taking a single blow. Instead, her blood is all over that warehouse. She's not strong enough to face Mikhail. Not as she is."

Adrian sucked in a breath through his teeth. "Don't let her hear you say that or you might lose all your chances of winning her back."

While I appreciated his optimism, I couldn't bring myself to share it. Not if I wanted to cling to my last shred of hope that he might someday be right.

"If it comes down to Kat surviving this hunt and her talking to me again? You know my answer, Adrian."

His expression turned serious. "You know what it would cost you."

My soul—however much of it was left. My memories. My lingering humanity.

Don't get involved in the human world.

Death's one rule, where every infraction meant a fond farewell to another piece of myself. A step too far, and I would become a shadow of what I was. Collecting souls without thought. Without any emotional connections or awareness of the world.

Without Kat.

I swallowed hard, but nodded. "To keep her safe, I'd give everything. Whatever the price."

23

Katerina

B ARRETT AND I had only just returned to the car when my phone rang. All I wanted to do was crawl into bed and sleep, maybe stuff my face with carbs. When I saw Maera's name on the screen, the promise of rest flitted away.

Getting my groan out first, I answered with a calm, "Is everything all right?"

Given the hour, now past midnight, I guessed the answer would be a resounding "no," but I wasn't expecting to hear my housekeeper's voice trembling so badly I struggled to understand her. "I need you to come home."

My heart made its way into my throat. "What's wrong?"

"It's Rhys. I don't know what's happening."

"Tell me."

He'd sounded fine if tired when he'd called me this morning, but I knew how quickly life could change. A sense of disassociation swept over me, my limbs feeling numb and detached as I braced for the worst.

"He slept in this morning." Her tone hit the note of *nothing new there*, knowing I'd understand. "When he woke up, he seemed off. Said he felt like he was coming down with something. And then—I can't describe it, Kat. It's like his brain has been rebooting the entire day. We'll be talking, and his eyes will fade to white, and then he'll come back. He says he's Seeing things. Flashes of visions. Like his second sight is going haywire. He hasn't eaten anything. He crawled back into bed around eight o'clock, and it's still going on. I'm afraid—I don't know what to do."

The need to track down Mikhail warred against my wish to be home with Rhys and Maera. Mikhail was hiding somewhere in this city, every hour getting closer to his grand finale, and I was no closer to finding him than I'd been when I arrived.

I hated the thought of turning my back on him, but until I had another lead, I was spinning my wheels. And if that was the case, I could spin them well enough at home while I figured out what was happening with Rhys. Was it a coincidence his second sight was on the fritz in the middle of our Mikhail fiasco, or was it somehow linked?

"I'll call Adrian and catch the next flight," I said. "It'll be all right, Maera. We won't let anything happen to him." I hung up and squeezed my phone in my hand. "Take me to the airport." Barrett looked at me. "Please."

He pulled onto the highway, and I tried to relax. When that failed, I called Adrian.

"Katerina, cuore mio, how did it go tonight? I understand you missed Mikhail?"

I glanced at Barrett, confused. Then anger sank in. Barrett hadn't had a chance to make any calls since we'd left the warehouse, which meant my old friend had been playing gossip with someone else.

"Next time Emrick swings by, tell him to butt out," I said. "But that's not why I'm calling. Can you call Maera? Rhys is having problems with his visions—they're in overdrive, and he's not coping well. Barrett's taking me to the airport, and I'm heading home."

"What about Mikhail?" Adrian's tone was curious, not accusing, but even so, I flinched.

"I know. The timing is awful. But maybe taking a step away will help me get a better perspective on trapping him. By the way, have you heard anything about some patron Mikhail's been working with? Powerful witch."

"I haven't, but I can look into it. As for Rhys, forget the airport. Barrett can drive you home."

Horrifying thought. "I'd prefer to fly. Barrett can go home to you." Where both Barrett and I preferred him to be.

"Don't be stubborn, Katerina. It will be hours before the next flight, and you could be on the island already."

I hated when he was right. The earliest flight I could catch would be around seven o'clock, two hours after I would be home if I stayed in the car with Mr. Grumpy Pants.

Barrett removed the choice from me when he zipped past our exit.

"While you're driving, I'll call Maera and do my best to keep her calm," Adrian continued. "I'll also reach out to some people to get a better idea of what's going on with the poor boy. As soon as I hear back from them, I'll be in touch."

I hung up, squeezed my eyes shut, and prayed Adrian's people found answers quickly. With Rhys's brain working so hard and so quickly without letting him sleep, he was at risk of frying his wires. I had little experience with second sight, but I'd known more than one psychic who'd lost control of their visions and never found their way back to the present. I had no idea how to help him, but I wouldn't let him or Maera go through this alone.

Nothing could happen to Rhys. Not only because he was my housekeeper's son, but because, in so many ways, he represented everything I'd once dreamed my own son could be.

The memory of deep blue eyes smiling up at me pierced my heart, and I swallowed the tears that threatened to choke me. I had failed Rowan, but I would do everything in my power to help Rhys through this.

"Tony got back to me while you were on the phone with Maera," Barrett said, and I might have hugged him for the distraction if he hadn't been driving. Or Barrett.

"And? What did the witch hunter have to say for himself?"

"They underestimated the fuck-up that is Toronto traffic."

The laugh that burst out of me was so bitter, it left fuzz on my tongue. "You can't be serious."

His mouth was a flat line. "So he says."

"You have theories?"

"I think they knew you were involved and wanted to make their opinion of you known. You say you don't need them—they wanted to prove you wrong."

"And now so many people are dead because of them." I shook my head in disgust. "Then they wonder why I think so little of them."

Barrett shrugged. "I guess you have a choice to make. If you plan on retiring, they'll be the only ones left to take your place."

I bit down hard on my tongue to keep myself from snapping back. I was going to be stuck in the car with this guy for the next six hours. The last thing I needed was an extra headache.

Instead, I turned on the radio and cranked the volume, then I sat back and let the scenery rush by as I headed home.

One benefit of driving in the middle of the night was the lack of traffic. We made it to the island within five hours, and I rushed into the house, leaving Barrett to make his way behind me.

Maera met me in the foyer, wringing her hands and looking over her shoulder.

"Any change?" I asked.

"He managed to sleep on and off for the past few hours, but the visions are still coming a few an hour."

I looked her over. Her red hair with its spattering of white flew in all directions from her fraying braid, and the circles under her eyes were as dark as black coffee. "You, on the other hand, haven't slept at all."

"How could I? My baby boy is—" Her chin wobbled, but she caught herself and pulled her shoulders back. "I know he'll be fine. I just hate not knowing how to help."

The woman was lying through her teeth with that first bit, but I wasn't about to argue with her.

"He's in his room?"

She nodded, and I kicked off my boots and made my way downstairs.

"Adrian called," she said as she followed me. "According to his Seer friends, what Rhys is going through is unusual. It could be a sign that his ability is getting stronger or that whatever he's trying to See is too big or too intense to get a good impression."

Considering everything that had gone down in Toronto over the past two days, I was inclined to lean towards the latter. Or maybe that was just what I hoped. If Rhys's ability was developing, it meant Maera and I would have no choice but to let him step fully into my world so he could get the help he needed. Neither of us were ready for that change.

I pushed open the door to Rhys's room, which stank of teenage boy though it was surprisingly tidy. The window was open a crack, letting the cool February wind flow in. Soft light seeped from the lamp on the bedside table, highlighting the shadows across Rhys's face.

He tossed and turned in bed, his face relaxing one moment only to scrunch up the next as he wrestled with whatever his brain was trying to show him.

I sank onto the mattress beside him and took his hand.

"Barrett will need somewhere to stay," I said to Maera, keeping my attention on Rhys. "If you wouldn't mind?"

"Of course." She hesitated in the doorway, then headed back upstairs.

Rhys stilled again, and I squeezed his hand, letting him know he wasn't alone.

His eyelashes fluttered, and he blinked his eyes open. From what Maera had described, I expected them to be white, but his usual present-seeing eyes stared back at me.

"Kat?"

"Hey, you."

"Why aren't you in Toronto?" His eyes widened. "Did you get him?"

"Not yet," I said, hating to disappoint him. "Came close, though."

His breath caught. He pressed his hand to his head and let out a low groan, and as I watched, his eyes went white.

"Blood. Always more blood. So much of it. It's like the whole world is bleeding. And you're about to drown in it."

24

Katerina

Aᴛ ᴛᴇʀ Rʜʏs's ᴍɪɴɪ-ᴠɪsɪᴏɴ, he fell back into a restless sleep. I stayed beside him, considering his words, his condition, and our next steps.

He couldn't stay like this. My worries about him burning out his circuits seemed all too well founded now that I'd seen him for myself.

Unfortunately, I hadn't heard from Adrian yet, so either there was no solution or I'd have to reach out to my own contacts.

Right now, the only person I could think of was Poppy. Whatever issues I had with her, she was the only witch I knew who might help.

I chewed on the side of my thumb, then shook off my doubts and opened my text messages.

Me: Second sight causing trouble. Needs a break. Any suggestions? Consider this the start of your redemption.

Minutes passed as I waited for her response. Finally, three little dots popped up. Then disappeared. Then popped up, then disappeared.

My patience hung by a thread, and I was about ready to call the woman when her reply came through. A recipe. Simple. Three ingredients Maera probably had in the kitchen, and one that made me raise an eyebrow.

Me: Hops? Really?

3rd Strike: Puts 'em right to sleep.

I had my doubts that a mundane tea would do much, but it was worth a shot. None of the ingredients were dangerous, so at least I didn't need to waste time sending a warning message about what I'd do to her if Rhys came to harm.

After pressing a kiss to Rhys's sweaty brow, I headed upstairs. Maera and Barrett sat at the kitchen table drinking coffee. A third cup sat steaming at an empty seat.

"This might let Rhys get some rest," I said, handing Maera my phone.

She glanced at the recipe, then rose from her seat and got to work.

Barrett frowned at me, and I read the question in his eyes. I didn't want Maera second-guessing herself about the sleeping potion, so I hoped my confident nod would be enough to keep him quiet until she'd left the room.

Spoilers: it wasn't.

"Did you get that from the witch?" he asked, his tone heavy with the full weight of his suspicion of all things magic. Was he trying to see how far he could push me?

I pressed my lips together, but at the counter, Maera stilled. "What witch?"

"Someone I know," I said. "She knows her stuff."

"She knows how to raise the dead and screw people over," Barrett said. "And she hates you."

"She also knows her potions and that to mess with me will get her killed," I shot back.

"All the more reason for her to enjoy some revenge."

"She can get in line."

A loud smash echoed throughout the room as Maera slammed a mug into the kitchen sink. I spun in my chair to face her, but she kept her back to me, her shoulders hunched as she leaned against the counter.

"Maera, trust me," I said. "You know I would never suggest anything that would put Rhys in danger. He needs to sleep."

"He needs to block his second sight," she said. "He can't keep going like this."

Something in the way she said it made my muscles tense. "What do you mean?"

Maera's shoulders hunched further, as though she were bracing herself.

"Maera?"

"I have watched him waste away month after month for years, and I can't do anything to stop it. From the time of his first vision, he's been slipping away from me, fading into himself with no idea how to navigate wherever he's going. He's lost his friends, he can't hold a job, and now his health—it has to stop, Katerina."

She finally turned to face me, and her eyes were full of fire. Not my kind of fire, but just as primal. The love of a mother for her only child. My heart clenched.

"Up until now, I have supported him the best I can, encouraging him to remember his visions, learn them so he can control them, but this is too much. If my encouragement has led him to this—if he can't—"

She pressed her lips together.

I rose to my feet and moved towards her, but she held up her hand to fend me off. "As of now, he's done with you. Adrian can help him find a way to block his visions, and Rhys can go back to having a regular, mundane life. No more magic, no more getting involved in your problems. I won't watch him suffer just to follow in your footsteps."

My throat closed as guilt overpowered me, and I closed my eyes to fight it back. In so many tiny ways, I'd encouraged Rhys's interest. Maybe we would have reached this point either way, but I hated the thought that he was in danger because of me.

I didn't know what bothered me more—that Maera was trying to cut out her son's gift as though it were a curse or that she believed I would be so reckless with his life.

Not that I didn't understand where she was coming from. She wanted to protect him. Keep him away from the hell on earth I'd encountered more than once during her lifetime—fewer than the number of times I'd walked through the flames before her, but enough to give her nightmares about what it would mean for Rhys if he continued down this path.

But as much as she didn't want to believe it, removing him from the magical world wouldn't protect him. It would only stifle his potential.

"You know how much he means to me, Maera. I would never leave him defenceless."

"You think you can promise that?" she asked. "Look at Barrett's face. Those gashes in his cheek weren't there the last time I saw him. And what about you? You may be almost healed, but don't think I didn't notice the way you dragged yourself in here as though you could barely stand. Rhys isn't like you two. He doesn't know how to fight. He can't summon fire or heal quickly. If cutting his ties to your world is the only way to ensure he lives a long, healthy life, then so be it."

How could I argue with her? She was only voicing the thoughts I'd carried since he was fifteen and first expressed an interest in joining me on a hunt.

And yet all I could think about was Rowan and how I would feel if he'd grown up without magic in his blood. After all, hadn't my parents left me behind when they'd gone out to clear the hills around Palonia of the wyverns and kelpies? Hadn't I always been told I wasn't able to defend myself so I would be a liability to the hunters?

Their lack of faith in me, and the expectations I'd heaped on myself, had prevented me from learning how to control my magic and isolated me from my community.

I didn't want to think about what would happen to Rhys if his mother tried to bind him. He might be able to adopt the mundane life Maera wanted, but I suspected the severed ties to his second sight wouldn't fade with time. They'd remain out of reach, an itch he was never able to scratch.

It would drive him mad.

But Maera was in no place to hear reason right now. First, we had to get him through this crisis.

"Whatever you think of my ability to keep Rhys safe, you know I would never suggest you give him something that would hurt him. You know these ingredients—at worst, they'll do nothing but help him relax. At best, he'll sleep. While we're arguing, he's suffering."

Maera's eyes flashed. "Don't you dare tell me what he needs. What do you know? You checked out of this world so long ago, I don't know if you understand what harm is anymore. All you care about is swatting problems away so you can go back to your Muskoka chair and pretend you don't exist. Is Rhys just another problem for you to swat away, Kat?"

I swallowed my irritation and did my best to keep my voice quiet. "Of course not. You're not wrong. I've been out of touch. I know that. But I would never—"

"You keep saying never, except you *are*. Don't you see that? If I'd been smart, I would have walked out on you years ago."

"Then why didn't you?" I snapped. "The door's always been right there."

Even as I said it, my heart pinched with pain. The thought of coming home to an empty house after every hunt. Spending my evenings alone, in silence. No video games on the TV downstairs, no music in the kitchen while Maera baked. I put so much effort into not hanging everything on the mortals in my life, knowing how briefly their time was with me, but the idea of going on without them left me cold.

She grimaced. "This is what I'm talking about. If it's so easy to watch us leave, then what faith can I have in you to make the best decisions for my son?"

My shoulders sagged. "Maera, I—"

"I stayed for you. And because I believed it was best for us. Just like you would have done what was best for Rowan."

I sucked in a breath and blinked through the stars that danced across my vision. The pain of her words nearly dropped me. Everything I wished I could have done to protect him. Everything I'd missed out on because I hadn't done enough.

Maera paused as though she knew she'd gone a step too far, but then she shook her head. "If you can't pull your head out of your ass and step back into this world, then it's time for me to reassess. Because if anything happens to him—"

"Him being me," Rhys said, and the two of us jumped and turned towards the stairs. Barrett stared at me, seemingly unsurprised by Rhys's sudden appearance. Had he heard him come upstairs while Maera and I argued? Were his muscles so thick they blocked his ability to flinch? I didn't know which answer was more likely.

"Rhys, what are you doing up?" Maera asked, rushing over to him and helping him to a chair at the table.

"I woke up and heard you yelling. Thought I'd better show my face before this fight came to blows."

I forced a chuckle through my fading grief. "Come on, Rhys, you know I wouldn't let it get that far. Your mother has a mean right hook and would take me down in a heartbeat."

No humour lit his green eyes. "You shouldn't be fighting about me at all. Not without giving me a chance to throw my opinions into the ring. I'm not a child or some plastic fortune-telling machine you find at the fair. I'm me. And I want to help. Mum, you can't block my visions."

She bowed her head with a sigh, then pulled her shoulders back. The two of them stared at each other with their matching green eyes and similar stubborn expressions.

"They're hurting you, Rhys," she said. "I won't stand by and let it happen."

"Then stand beside me and help me figure it out," he replied. He squeezed his eyes shut and pinched the bridge of his nose. Maera and I froze, waiting to make sure he was all right. The moment passed, and he looked at his mother. "Since my first visions, I've been all over the place with them, wanting them gone, wanting them stronger, wanting to understand where they come from. I know now that what I want is to master them. They're not going anywhere, and the more I try to ignore them, the worse they get. I've been trying to find answers on my own, trying to teach myself how to remember, and obviously that's not going well, so I think it's time for a change. I need help. And then, after I get the hang of my Sight, I want to find a way to use it."

I met Maera's eye across the table, watched the way the woman seemed to crumble at her son's announcement, and she dropped into the chair beside him. "I understand why you want to, Rhys, but you don't know what's out there."

The line of his jaw hardened. "That's just it, Mum, I do. I See it. I've Seen what Mikhail will do if he gets his way, and it's terrifying. If I can help stop him, I've got to do it, or I won't be able to look at myself. All the death and destruction in my head will sit there, reminding me how I failed. Don't you get that?"

She hesitated for a moment, then dropped her chin in a nod. "I do. I hate it, but I do."

Rhys turned to me. "So will you let me help?"

Just like Maera, I couldn't answer right away. I knew what saying yes would lead to—not only sharing what he Saw while he waited around at home, but joining me in my hunt for Mikhail as an extra set of hands—or eyes—in a fight. My stomach dropped at the idea of him being in the thick of it with me. I didn't want him to get hurt.

But if Rhys's premonitions were true—and so far they'd been horribly accurate—blood was going to run if we didn't stop Mikhail. He'd outsmarted me at every turn, and my resources were tissue-paper thin. I needed all the help I could get.

"All right, Rhys," I said, though I felt like Emrick, giving up a piece of my soul with the words. "Why don't we start by going through everything you remember and see if we can piece it together?"

25

Katerina

BY THE TIME we'd worked through all of Rhys's recent visions—during which he'd had two more flashes—we had a notepad covered in scribbles, a very clear idea of how Rhys's visions had progressed through Mikhail's goings-on, and very little idea what his next move might be.

Rhys's exhaustion overpowered his disappointment that he hadn't remembered more, and it took another interrupted nap to push Maera into whipping up Poppy's recipe.

Within fifteen minutes, Rhys had returned downstairs and was passed out on the rec room couch. Maera wished us a good night—at nine o'clock in the morning—and sought out her own bed, leaving me and Barrett at the kitchen table.

Doubts, fears, and stresses bombarded me whenever I dropped my guard. The argument with Maera had left a bad taste in my mouth, and although I'd heard from one of Adrian's Seer friends, their email hadn't left me feeling confident. According to them, Rhys was likely suffering a vision storm—too many coming in at once without the training to slow them down or sort them out. They recommended something to help him sleep and reassured me the storm would pass. Though they quickly followed up their reassurances by saying that without proper training, the storms would happen more often and likely get worse, leading to severe and possibly permanent disassociation from the present.

No pressure.

Running beneath all that was my fear that we would miss our chance to stop Mikhail before he carried out the next phase of his plan.

To keep my hands busy and see what else I could tease from Rhys's glimpses into the future, I set about rewriting the scribbles in an orderly list. Witches in a circle. Bodies piling up. Nothing vivid.

The blood entered the scene later on, according to Maera. Brief mentions, but not enough to make her sit up and take notice. After all, blood magic wasn't rare among even the greyest of witches. Blood was simply a powerful medium. Whether it crossed into dark magic came down to the willingness of the donor.

The vision I'd come home to a few days ago had been the most graphic and disturbing, but the ones he'd suffered in the past twenty-four hours hadn't been pretty. It didn't take a psychic to know Mikhail wasn't going to stop any time soon. Not until he got whatever he was after.

Which was still a giant unknown.

I groaned and bowed my head into my hands.

"What?" Barrett asked, and I jumped.

I'd honestly forgotten he was there. While I had no desire to deal with his grumpiness right now, bouncing some ideas around sounded better than running circles in my head.

"I'm trying to decide what to do with all this." I shoved the notepad away. The scribbles were making me cranky. "Unless Poppy hears something else, which I doubt, our only lead has told me everything she knows."

"We could go back to that witch at Rune the Day," Barrett suggested. "What was her name? Raisa?"

"She's more likely to send me into another trap. We could find a way to use her, though. Maybe give the witch hunters a chance to redeem themselves."

"Follow where Raisa goes and crash her next coven meeting?"

I shook my head. "Our crashing days are over, I think. Going forward, Mikhail will expect me to show up at every event. We need to find a way to set him off balance, or we won't catch him. The man is a pain in my ass. For forty years, I've watched him get away with literal murder. I've been around so much longer than he has, yet he's always acted like he *knows* me."

Barrett's expression shuttered. He sat back in his chair, crossed his arms, and glared at me.

In the face of all my self-doubt, his attitude rubbed me the wrong way. To stop myself from being bowled over by it, I opted to push back and mirrored his pose. "What is it now? Am I unimpressing you again with my lack of ingenuity?"

"This is what I hate about you magic users," he said, his tone bland. "You're sitting here talking about how this killer is a thorn in your side, talking about the evil he's committed like he's some competition trying to put you out of business. He's dealing in *lives* here, Katerina."

A prickle of anger scurried up my spine and left a haze on the edges of my vision. "You think I don't know that? Why do you think I've been busting my ass for the past two days?"

"Is that what this is? Because it looks a lot like you're dragging your feet to avoid finding him."

Guilt, frustration, and the deeper worry that he was right nearly overwhelmed me. "I haven't heard you coming up with any better ideas, Mr. Tactician."

"Would you have taken them if I did?"

"Try me. Throw one at me right now. What are we supposed to do next?"

"We go back to Toronto and talk to Raisa. Or someone from any of the other covens we know is involved. More than one witch bolted when we raided that warehouse, which tells me not everyone is as sold on Mikhail's message as the rest. They're the ones we need to talk to."

I hated his cold practicality. His belief that he had all the answers while I was some emotional, inexperienced nothing. "And how do we find out who they are, hm? Go door to door asking where their allegiances lie?"

His dark eyes flashed, and his shoulders climbed towards his ears. "See?"

I scowled. Of course he took my argument as a rejection. He was so certain he was right he couldn't see the flaws in his so-called plan. If we had all the time in the world to waste, then sure, I'd start tomorrow. It wouldn't be the first time I'd turned to classic legwork on a hunt. But Mikhail wouldn't give us the space to find what we needed. Especially not now that we'd shown our hand. He would race against us before we had time to get our bearings. We'd have more luck going door to door in every warehouse district than tracking down a witch willing to talk.

Barrett shook his head. "If I hadn't pulled you back, you would have run into that meeting the same way you ran into the shop basement. You're acting like you hold all the power, but from what I've seen, you're a hack who should have retired years ago. Maera's right—you need to make up your mind. Are you the sorceress who vowed to protect this world from whatever magical dangers threaten it or not? Because this in-between bull-shit you've been pulling isn't helping anyone. It's just giving us more of a mess to clean up."

I clenched my teeth to stop myself from snapping back. But if I stayed silent, he'd believe he was right.

And he wasn't.

Was he?

Swallowing my pride, setting that question aside to ask myself later, I said, "Fine. Make a list of places we can hit. After we get some sleep, we'll head back to Toronto and start asking around. Call Tony and get him to send people he trusts to do their own snooping. They might not know where Mikhail spends his time, but I refuse to believe they aren't paying attention when he steps into the open."

Our silent standoff stretched out until Barrett nodded. "I'll reach out to him. We can leave tonight."

He rose from the table and strode towards the guest room where Maera had stashed him. I made a face at his back, then headed for my own room.

Only when the door closed behind me and the silence of the house enveloped me did I bow my head against the door and wonder at what point I'd become such a failure.

26

Emrick

Aᴌᴍᴏsᴛ ꜰɪꜰᴛᴇᴇɴ ʜᴜɴᴅʀᴇᴅ years collecting magical souls, and it never failed to disgust me how cruel people could be to each other.

Seven corpses lay on the floor, eyes open and unseeing, expressions contorted in horror. There was blood everywhere.

This sort of carnage wasn't limited to magicals, but the creativity when magic was involved… it could still surprise me.

Except this destruction struck me as familiar.

As I stepped from one body to the next, resting my hand on bare skin to watch the corpse crumble to dust beneath my touch, I assessed the victims to try to remember where I'd seen this particular brand of death before.

Unlike the three I'd stumbled on in the office building the other day, these people showed no sign of direct violence. No knife wounds, no defensive wounds. If anything, their injuries were superficial.

And yet they were covered in blood. As though someone had taken a spray bottle and coated them with it.

Another memory nagged at me, but again when I went to grab it, it disappeared.

Frustrated, I pulled on my leather gloves so I wouldn't dust the final corpse and knelt beside her. Carefully, I tugged the bottom hem of her

T-shirt up to see the expanse of skin across her stomach. More blood under her clothes, as though she'd bled through her pores. Nasty tears along the surface of her skin, with smaller scrapes in between them where she seemed to have scratched herself raw.

Another ping of memory.

Following the trail, I picked up the witch's hand and inspected her fingers. Sure enough, the blunt fingernails with their chipped purple polish were caked with torn skin and more blood.

I set her hand down and shifted my attention to her face. Her lips were bloodless, blending so well with her ashen skin I would have missed them had I not been staring right at them.

Just like the other three witches, the seven here had been drained. More expertly this time. With magic instead of mundane weapons.

Her blue eyes reminded me so much of Katerina's my heart skipped a beat, and another piece of the missing memory fell into place.

The last time I'd seen this sort of death, I'd been with her.

Horror filled me, and I jerked away from the corpse and backed up until I hit the wall and was able to see the room as a whole.

No, I hadn't been with Kat. I'd been working. Clearing body after body after body, wading through a gory scene that had stayed with me for decades after I walked away. Centuries. Of course it had. My life had changed forever that day.

I took in the spray of blood, the way it misted across the floor towards a central location in the middle of the room, towards a noticeably clean spot. As though someone had stood there, accepting the sacrifice.

My stomach turned as I pulled off my glove and turned the final corpse to dust. I had to tell Kat about this, and I did not look forward to her reaction. In fact, I'd never been more afraid of anything in my life.

I was going to need Adrian's help.

27

Katerina

T TOOK ME ages to fall asleep.

Every time I closed my eyes, I saw Mikhail laughing at me. Or those witches dead on the floor. Or my parents looking at me with deep disappointment, holding my son out of reach.

And as I'd watched the shadows shift across my wall, the winter sun catching the empty branches outside my balcony, I'd considered how much I deserved the punishment of such cruel thoughts. It had been a long time since I'd gone on a hunt this intense, and I was flailing, blowing about with every breeze. Every time I thought I'd gotten my footing, the ground gave out beneath me.

I felt weak. Small. Useless.

When I'd mastered my magic so many centuries ago, I'd sworn to myself I would never again feel small. I'd promised my dead parents I would pick up where they'd left off so I would never again feel useless.

My reputation as a force to be reckoned with wasn't based on nothing. I *had* been the best hunter out there. Adrian, Emrick, and I had stopped more disasters than the modern witch hunters could blink at.

But I'd let exhaustion, depression, and loneliness wear down my magic and my self-image. I was a husk of the sorceress I'd been, and I didn't know if I had the energy to thicken my skin and earn back what I'd lost.

By the way Barrett talked to me, the way Raisa and the witches in the warehouse had reacted to me, they knew it.

Maera knew it. She encouraged me to brush off the dust and get back to work as though she believed this was a passing phase I could break out of, but honestly, I didn't know how. This apathy had been a ball and chain around my ankle for so long, and other than making sure Mikhail didn't carry out some great evil, I had no drive to change. All I had to look forward to were more long years, each one promising the same rotation of companions, the same loss, the same challenges.

It was enough to make me want to curl up and sleep for the next millennium. Not like it'd kill me.

On that thought, I'd fallen asleep, but my outlook wasn't much brighter when I woke up.

I dragged myself out of bed and into the shower. While the hot water pattered on the crown of my head, I mulled over Barrett's plan, which didn't seem any smarter now than it had before. At the same time, I saw his point. At least knocking on doors was better than sitting around waiting for answers to fall into our laps.

Clean, moderately rested, and eager to find out how Rhys was doing, I pulled on a dark green sweater and a pair of black leggings and went into the kitchen.

My stomach grumbled at the sight of pancakes covered in fruit and syrup waiting for me. Barrett had already devoured half of his, and I was shocked—shocked!—to see the man eating something as sweet as syrup. Considering his apparent inability to enjoy anything in life, I would have expected him to eat nothing more extravagant than a tangerine around the holidays. But only one.

"I thought you'd forgotten," he said in greeting.

"That I have the privilege of spending another six hours cooped up in a moving box with you? Never."

I dropped into my seat and drizzled syrup over the pancakes. "Has Rhys woken up yet?"

Maera shook her head and poured coffee into three mugs. She sprinkled a dash of cinnamon on top of mine, and I took it as the act of reconciliation it was. "Still sleeping. I checked on him when I woke up, though, and he seems to be all right."

By the time I finished my last pancake, making as many yummy noises as possible to return Maera's gesture of peace, the sounds of a video game reached us from downstairs. Not a good sign. Especially not when the smell of coffee and pancakes would normally send him running.

"I'll go see," I said.

Maera looked ready to argue with me, but she turned her attention to the empty plates instead. "Tell him there's a stack waiting for him."

I headed downstairs and found Rhys sitting on the rec room couch. The TV screen was a wash of colour and movement as he navigated his way through his sneaky-stabby adventure, but as soon as I sat beside him, he paused the game and turned to face me.

"I had dreams," he said.

"Vision-type dreams or regular-type dreams?"

He set down the controller and scrubbed his hands over his face. "I don't know. I don't think they were visions. They didn't feel… itchy in my brain the way visions do. But they were more than dreams. If that makes sense."

I shrugged. "None of this makes sense, Rhys. Life is a whirlwind of confusion. But maybe you're right that it was somewhere in the middle. Some people say dreams are our way of processing memories. Maybe your brain took all your visions, the ones you don't remember well, and assembled them into a more coherent picture while you slept?"

He picked at the seam of the couch. "Maybe. But if that's the case, it was definitely more nightmare than dream."

I took a second to make myself comfortable on the soft cushions.

"Do you really think I'll be in danger if I learn how to control my Sight?" he asked. The question came so quietly, I had to strain to catch it.

"I don't know. I hope not. But I suppose it will depend on your choices." I rested my crossed arms on my knees. "If it were up to me and your mother, you would stay far away from my battles and only help by sharing your visions. What scares us is that we know you too well. We know that won't be enough for you."

He sank back into the cushions. "I want to help," he said, his youthful earnestness pooling in every syllable. "How can anyone who knows what's out there sit back and do nothing?"

Although I knew he didn't mean it as an accusation, I felt the question as a slap. As a vicious reminder of everything I'd once felt and believed. He was right. However much I wanted to turn my back on the monsters prowling through the world, ignoring them wouldn't make them go away. It would only let them win.

I massaged the knots in the back of my neck and did my best to put my thoughts in order.

"We'll get through this, Rhys. Step by step. I promise. We won't leave you floundering in the dark. Unfortunately, leaning into these visions means picking the nightmares apart so we can get to the root of them. Do you think you're ready to do that?"

He paled, but his jaw tightened with determination. "I am."

"All right, then. What exactly did you See? Walk me through every last detail. Remember I'm here with you, and tell me when you need a break."

Rhys took a deep breath, closed his eyes, and for a full minute sat in silence. I watched, waited, hoped the details hadn't been lost in the rush of waking up. When he opened his eyes again, they were filled with certainty, and the muscles in my neck relaxed. We were good.

"I'm sorry if it's not everything you need to know," he said, "but I don't want to accidentally throw in details I *think* I remember, you know what I mean?"

"I do. The brain has a way of filling in the gaps. Just tell me what you Saw, and we'll go from there. Any new information is useful information."

He closed his eyes again and settled into the couch. "There's a group, hooded, sitting in a circle. An intense sense of power. Someone at the head of the circle with their hands raised. In the middle of the circle is a pot. There's steam coming out of it." He opened his eyes and frowned. "Makes it sound like some kind of weird cooking circle, doesn't it?"

I offered him a wry smile. "That's pretty much the foundation of most witchcraft, Rhys. Sorry to disappoint you."

"This would be a lot less terrifying if that were actually the case."

His haunted expression nearly pushed me to end the conversation there. I didn't want him reliving the trauma of whatever he'd Seen. But we would be doing ourselves a disservice if I stopped him. Rhys needed to get these thoughts out of his head so he wasn't suffering them alone, and I needed to know what his second sight was showing him. As awful as it was, the only way for either of us to move past this point was to get through it.

"Let's pause for a moment," I said. "Can you make out anything about the circle? Any markings on the floor? What about the colour of whatever's in the pot?"

"Nothing on the floor, and I can't make out anything through the steam. Maybe pink? I don't know. It could be the light. It's like there's a... glow around everything. But it's coming from a source. Through a window, maybe?"

"That's good. Any details you pick out might help us pinpoint where they are."

Rhys raised his eyebrow. "With that much pink, you think it's next to a strip club?"

I shrugged. "Could be. What better place to hide? No one would look your way for a few loud noises."

We shared a smile, and I nodded for him to keep going.

After he pulled himself together and released another big breath, he took me through the rest of his dream. Every new description added to the picture being painted. The growing number of witches, the room becoming crowded, the air thick with steam from the pot. The light from outside shifting. Pink. Blue. Yellow. Always at night.

The person at the head of the circle remained where they were, but often a second person joined them, someone even the first person bowed to.

Was one of them Mikhail and the other his mysterious patron? Who was the bower and who the bowee? I wished these witches weren't so dramatic with their hooded cloaks. They were alone in a room with each other—what were they hiding from?

"There was something else," Rhys said, his brow furrowing in concentration, as though straining to remember would bring the details back. "Something else about this scene that's not here now."

"Don't force it. Take a deep breath, relax."

"Screams."

Maera's voice drew our attention to the bottom of the stairs. I had no idea how long she'd stood there, but by the pinched expression on her face, I guessed a while. As soon as we spotted her, she approached the couch and dropped onto the other side of the sectional.

"He said he heard screams."

Rhys's frown deepened. "Why can't I remember that?"

"I've never heard you mention sounds before," I said. "Maybe your other senses aren't as clear in your vision state? So you remember what you see, but nothing else?"

He snorted. "That's not helpful, is it?"

I patted his hand. "Don't stress. You've told me a lot." I turned to Maera. "Did he say anything else?"

"Fireworks?" she said. "That one didn't make sense to me. In context of all the blood, I wondered if he'd actually heard gunshots, but he kept saying fireworks."

"Maybe that's the flashing lights?" I suggested.

Rhys shook his head. "The lights were steady, changing every few seconds."

"We'll come back to the fireworks, then. Anything else?" I asked Maera.

"'Stop, please, make it stop.'" She spoke in a monotone, but the bleak look in her eyes told me Rhys hadn't said it nearly as calmly. Probably at a volume and in a tone no mother wanted to hear from her child.

Rhys blanched. "Yes. Make it stop." He rubbed at his arms. "Stop. It has to stop."

Maera pointed at him. "That's what you said. And you made the same gesture." She rubbed her arms to show what she meant.

A prickle of unease ran through me, and before I knew I was moving, I was on my feet. "Were you rubbing your arms like you were cold? Or were you scratching?"

A crowd of people. A pot in an open field. Steam bubbling from the surface.

Maera's gaze faded into the middle distance, but as I watched, her fingers curled in. "Scratching," she said. "Definitely."

Stop. Please. Make it stop. Fingernails tearing into arms. Legs. Face.

"He talked about absorbing power, taking strength from our enemies," Poppy

had said.

Screams. Blood. So much blood.

My tongue stuck to the roof of my mouth, dry and unwieldy. Black spots danced in my vision. I drew a breath in through my nose. "Rhys." Was that my voice shaking? I stretched out my fingers, then squeezed them into fists in an effort to ease the trembling. "Could your mum be right about the fireworks being gunshots? The corpses on the floor, did you see any injuries? Anything that could be gunshot wounds?"

Slowly, so slowly, he shook his head. "Nothing like that. Just the bodies on the floor covered in blood. Blood on the floor. Sprays of it." He stopped short and cocked his head to the side. "And one person standing in the middle of everyone. Covered in blood from head to toe but standing. Alive. A survivor?"

A laugh, not a little hysterical, bubbled inside me and spilled between my teeth, as shaky as my hands.

I wrapped my arms around my middle and stared out the floor-to-ceiling windows that looked over the backyard and down to the beach. Light streamed in from outside, mocking the darkness that had swept over my mind.

The stairs creaked, and a moment later, Barrett appeared at the bottom. Somehow I knew he'd been listening. Sitting on the stairs, maybe, or near the stairwell upstairs. He'd heard everything Rhys had said but hadn't wanted to interrupt. Or maybe he didn't want to get too close to the petty magical concerns.

But we'd stepped far beyond petty.

Unless I was mistaken, reading too much into a collection of vague details.

Surely all power-absorbing spells involved blood flying through the air. The scratching had to be a coincidence.

Yet even as I tried to convince myself there was no possibility of my suspicions being true, even as I crammed the idea under the soles of my feet in an attempt to ignore them and leave the way open for any other horrible explanation to occur to me, the temperature in the room dropped.

A chill ran down my spine in sharp contrast to the warm flush of anxiety that had taken hold on the back of my neck.

Mist crawled across the floor, and the tension in Emrick's shoulders as he stepped out of the afterlife confirmed everything I feared.

The world crashed down around me, setting the room reeling.

I was going to be sick.

"Kat?" Rhys asked.

Maera was already on her feet and reaching for me, and Barrett stepped forward. I ignored them, caught in the anguished expression in Emrick's silver eyes.

"Is it true?" I asked him.

He pressed his lips together, and his throat bobbed with a swallow.

Then he nodded. A subtle dip of his chin I might have missed if I weren't watching for it.

"Is what true?" Barrett asked.

I opened my mouth to answer, but all that came out was a squeak. I swallowed, tried again. "Mikhail's spell. The big plan he's working on? It's the same one the traitors in Palonia used to slaughter my family." I felt the sounds vibrating in my throat, heard my voice coming out, detached and distant. My pain lurked, sitting on the edge of my awareness, as I forced out the next words. "Mikhail is going to massacre these witches to become immortal."

28

Katerina

THE MOMENT THE words were out of my mouth, my stomach rebelled. Unable to speak, afraid to open my mouth in case my pancakes made a reappearance, I rushed to the stairs.

Maera and Rhys stared after me in horror, but Barrett didn't flinch. His unflappableness might have been reassuring if I weren't so flapped.

Memories tumbled over fears for the future as I attempted to process what it meant if Mikhail had found that ritual.

The ritual that was supposed to be lost.

The ritual Emrick and I had spent centuries trying to find so we could destroy it.

And Emrick knew.

My stomach twisted again, and I upped my pace, needing to get away from all these eyes so I could break down in private.

"Kat, are you—" Rhys called after me.

I waved my hand in response, but I didn't know what anyone thought I was trying to say. That I was fine? No one in this house would believe that.

"Kat," Maera started as I reached the top of the stairs, but a deeper voice murmured something, and she fell silent.

I knew who'd spoken, so I was less surprised and more frustrated when

I reached my room only to find Emrick waiting for me.

He stood there in his eternal perfection, a dark purple sweater setting off the otherworldly glow in his moonlight eyes. His gloved hands were tucked into the pockets of his dark jeans, giving him a relaxed appearance that belied the concern in his expression.

But as good as he looked today, I found myself staring at the man he'd been the morning we'd met. His blond hair had been longer and darker then, tied back with a leather strap with strands falling free across his high cheekbones. He'd had a thicker beard that lined his jaw, unlike the well-maintained stubble he wore now.

The eyes, though, were exactly the same.

Right down to the sympathy staring back at me when I looked into them.

Except today I wasn't standing in a blood-soaked field where the bonfires from last night's festival still burned. I wasn't standing in the ashes of my entire community, every last one of my people ripped from me for the sake of three women's dreams of eternal life.

Emrick pulled one hand from his pocket.

"Don't," I whispered, turning away from him to push the door open and step onto the balcony.

He followed, his closeness as tangible as a physical touch. It swept around me in a cocoon of love and support, and the warmth of it nearly broke me.

Memories bombarded me. The harder I tried to stem them, the faster they came.

"Come on, Kate, we're going to be late!"

My sister's giggling voice echoed in my head, urging me out the door of the single-room wattle-and-daub cottage we shared with my parents, grandmother, brothers, husband, and son.

So many details I would have sworn I'd forgotten. The sweet aroma of peat burning on the fire. The brisk wind whistling through the open door-way, rustling the straw beneath my feet. Sunlight shining through the single tiny window beside the door.

So early in the day, my husband, Shep, hadn't arrived yet. He and the other members of his team were out hunting a wyvern that had rampaged too close to a mundane village not far from Palonia. Word had reached us that morning that they'd been victorious with no losses, and tonight's harvest festival was as much a celebration of their success as the turn of the seasons.

My son, Rowan, bounced on my knee, draped in his linens. His blue eyes stared up at me with such glee that I couldn't help but laugh and bounce him again. He was why I was still sitting here instead of joining the rest of my community outside.

My son of nineteen months who'd only just learned how to put one foot in front of the other without falling.

A sob stuck in my throat, lodging in my diaphragm. I couldn't draw breath, couldn't push the sound through. Agony choked me, and I fell to my knees, but the memories kept coming.

The fires, my family, my Gran's crinkled smile. Shep arriving and wrap-ping his arms around me as though I were the best part of coming home, smelling of damp wool and fresh air with an undertone of dirt and sweat. Him sweeping Rowan off to watch the food being cooked.

So much life and love and closeness.

Alodie, Mae, and Blythe making their rounds with the foul drink that had Kyla and me laughing at how bad it was. Thinking the three sorceresses had messed up the recipe.

My first sight of Emrick across the fires, his eyes sharp and full of liquid moonlight.

How long after that had the screams begun?

So much screaming. I was far from my family when the itch set in. I'd fought against it, but my nails had found their way to my flesh, tearing at my arms, releasing the droplets of blood that rose into the air and floated to the women chanting around the pot set over one of the fires.

I rubbed at my arms, just as I had that night. All around me, my people had begged for an end to the pain. Somewhere in the crowd, my family had begged along with them, out of sight, suffering without my being there to hold them.

For so long, I'd held those memories at bay, but today they were a tidal wave about to knock me senseless.

Mikhail. Focus on Mikhail.

Don't think about how I hadn't been able to say goodbye.

Had never seen my son's beautiful smile again.

Never got to hold him or kiss him goodnight.

And I couldn't even follow him because I'd been too much of a coward to let myself die along with everyone else. I'd covered myself in a layer of thick frost and frozen myself to the ground. My failure to master my magic had pushed me to develop different skills from anyone else in Palonia, and in the end, that skill had saved me while every other sorcerer perished.

I'd saved myself while everyone around me died.

The shame—a torment—had remained as constant as my youth for almost nine hundred years.

My cries escaped me, and a wail filled my ears that only just covered the echoes of the past.

Solid arms encircled me, pulled me towards an equally solid chest. Between sobs, I breathed in Emrick's scent of campfire and loam, absorbed the heat that wafted off the man who had been there for me since I'd first come to terms with the repercussions of that ritual.

The spirit-herder who'd heard rumours about what those women had planned and had shown up early for his duty of escorting magical souls to the afterlife. He'd been curious to see if the trio would succeed.

He'd had no idea that by being there, the course of his future would shift forever.

I clung to him, wishing I had the strength to send him away to protect us both but too caught up in a current so strong and swift I couldn't find my footing without him.

Emrick was my anchor, not only to this world but to myself, and as my past crashed into my present, I was terrified of getting lost in the collision.

Gentle fingers stroked my hair, a firm hand rubbed my back, but he said nothing. Not a single word to offer comfort or soothe me, and I was more grateful for his silence than I could say.

With great effort, I pushed the thoughts of my tortured family away and wrenched my attention towards the three women who had been the cause of my suffering.

Alodie. Mae. Blythe. Three of my teachers. The fighter, the elder, and the healer. No one would have guessed they'd work together to wreak such carnage.

And for what?

By the time their ritual was complete, they'd been as dead as the rest.

I'd thought they'd failed.

Emrick had thought they'd failed.

Until he realized their spell had backfired and hit me instead as the sole survivor. Except I hadn't been bound to the demon the three had attempted to summon.

Maybe I would have been if Emrick hadn't been present.

Instead, my soul had linked with his.

Eternal life, eternal youth, but only so long as this man paid his debt to Death.

What could we expect if Mikhail attempted this ritual? Would he, too, be consumed by the power of the spell and perish, or would he complete the binding and gain the eternity he sought?

"We can't let him perform that ritual," I said through exhausted gasps as the fist squeezing my lungs slowly released its hold.

"We won't," Emrick murmured in my ear. "Whatever else happens, I promise you that. We won't let him succeed."

29

Katerina

THE MOMENT STRETCHED out. I knew I should pull away, but for the life of me, I couldn't bring myself to do it. I never felt more at home than when I was in Emrick's arms, and as the pieces of my heart threatened to spill across the floor, he was the only thing keeping me together.

But it would be too easy to fall back on old habits.

This was why I'd wanted to make a clean break from him—had worked so hard not to long for him for seventy-five years. I had no willpower when it came to him.

My skin warmed as his hand continued its gentle caress up and down my spine. My body begged to curl up close, to set these horrors aside by losing myself in the heat of his body. In passionate kisses that devoured my breath and panting moans that drove out all thought except for the pleasure only Emrick knew how to evoke.

My fingers curled around his arm, and his bicep flexed under my touch. His other arm tightened around me. Subtly, leaving space for me to escape, but drawing me in until his heart raced against mine. My hands itched to slide through his hair, to push him down to the floor and straddle his waist.

To drown in his moonlight eyes and block out the visions that bubbled and popped behind my eyelids like molten lava ready to erupt.

With immense effort, I pulled away and resisted looking at him, knowing the emotions I'd find there would shatter the fragile walls I struggled to hold in place. I had lost so much in my life that the idea of losing him too—permanently—was enough to break me. My only choice until we found a better solution was to distance myself from him. Even if it took all my strength to do it.

"Show me," I said.

"I don't know if that's a good idea."

I squeezed my hands into fists to crush the flames that flickered along with my anger. "I don't need you to protect me, Emrick. I need to see it for myself."

Tension radiated off him as though he were coiled to spring. Then he released a breath and pushed himself to his feet. "Come on, then."

He pulled off his glove and held out his hand. From my place on the floor, I slid my fingers through his, my skin buzzing to life as our hands made contact. I stood as the mist rose around us, and he brought us through the afterlife.

When the scene cleared, my heart stopped, and I forced myself to breathe through my mouth so the reek of blood didn't set off my gag reflex.

On a good day, blood didn't bother me. I would have been in the wrong line of work if it did. But there was so much of it. Red covered the floor, the walls, even the ceiling in a thick, layered spray. The windows on the far side of the room were spattered, and the sunlight shining through left dappled patterns across the floor.

Even with the corpses turned to dust, the acidic tang of the witches' terror lingered. Or maybe that was my imagination, more memories leaking through.

I turned in a slow circle. "How many were there?"

Emrick pulled his glove back on and shoved his hands in his pockets.

"Seven."

"Not enough for the full ritual."

Alodie, Mae, and Blythe had used three hundred sacrifices to reach their goal and had only succeeded in binding me. I doubted Mikhail would get away with seven.

"Another test run," Emrick agreed.

"A successful one by the look of it. We're not far from the grand finale."

My attention was caught by a satchel on the floor. Something about the red tassels dangling from the strap refused to let me look away. I moved towards it, the drying stickiness of the blood underfoot tearing at my fuzzy socks.

I recognized the bag.

A flash of angry eyes, a spell circle thrown at my head, no small amount of contempt.

Raisa.

Sighing, I bowed my head. I'd known better than to think she'd listen to my warnings. "This woman was so convinced Mikhail would deliver on his promises."

"To be fair, he did," Emrick said, his voice dripping with loathing.

I turned to look at him, my eye catching his before I could avoid it. And dammit, I'd been right. Concern, love, curiosity. He wanted to know how I was feeling, worried I was about to collapse again. He wanted to offer comfort and protect me from what was coming.

I saw it all in a glance, and my traitorous heart responded. It raced and skipped and fluttered against my ribs. No one understood what I was going through better than this man who'd been there the first time I'd fallen apart. Who'd stayed with me in my darkest moments and helped me piece myself back together.

Tearing my gaze away, I gave the room one last scan. It took me a moment to recognize the basement storeroom of Rune the Day. Not the warehouse Rhys had seen, not the place we were looking for.

Because that would have been too easy.

Mikhail probably knew I'd find these corpses; he wouldn't want to lead me right to him.

"You didn't find anything else?" I asked.

"Only the bodies."

I should have been pleased by Emrick's answer. He wasn't supposed to be digging into this mess. That would mean him getting involved in the mortal world, which would mean sacrificing another piece of his soul.

But damn, I could have used a leg up here.

I held out my hand, and Emrick's bare fingers closed around mine. As the scene disappeared, I realized how stuck I was. The sand was pouring ever faster through the hourglass, and we had no idea where to find Mikhail. We had to track down that warehouse, then come up with a solid plan. One that accounted for every no-show, every surprise angle.

We had to be prepared for hundreds of witches, all of them ready to fight to the death for what they believed was their best shot at immense power. That much magic, that much desperation—I would have been hard-pressed to fight against them even at the height of my ability.

Despite all the greater problems staring me down, only one question looped through my head, stuck on replay as my bedroom came into view.

"How is it possible, Emrick?" I asked. "We spent ages hunting for any trace of that spell. We never found it. Alodie, Mae, and Blythe took it with them when they died. I'm the only walking proof it ever existed. How did Mikhail learn it?"

I glanced at him over my shoulder, and my breath caught at the intensity staring back at me.

"Is that really all you have to say about this?" he asked softly. "Kate, you just walked in on your worst nightmare. How many decades did you wake up screaming, haunted by the thought of this exact thing happening?"

"Kat," I reminded him.

The lines around his mouth tightened. Some might have read irritation in his expression, but those people didn't know him as well as I did. I saw only his regret.

"Kat. Forgive me. You know as well as I do it's not easy to change a habit of centuries."

Centuries of words whispered in the dark. Names cried out between moans. Sweat-slicked skin and fiery kisses.

Never mind that I changed my name because, after he left, I hated that no one said it the way he did.

"As for the rest, the past is the past," I said. "Yes, this is a pretty awful walk down memory lane, but I can't let it distract me from the fact that one of the worst people in the world carries some scary-ass knowledge. How did he get it?"

"Does it matter?" he asked. "He has the spell. You need to stop him before he uses it."

"What if he's not the only one who knows it?" Even asking the question drained the blood from my face and left me reeling. "If this ritual is back in the world after so many centuries, how do we contain it?"

"There's only one person who knows for sure."

"Mikhail." His name came out like a curse, and I wished I carried that level of power within me. The idea of him keeling over wherever he was, suffering some kind of stabby pain in his guts as my hatred tore through him soothed the whirlwind rushing in my veins.

Unfortunately, I was caught in the same position I'd been in ten minutes ago. I had to find him.

Once I did, I had to pray I'd be enough to stop him.

"I'm going to need to bring out the big guns for this," I said.

The corner of Emrick's lips kicked up. "Tell me what you need."

I started to ask him for help. Centuries of working with him and Adrian had made it a default response to include him in all my preparations.

But I couldn't. It wouldn't be fair to either of us to ask him to stay.

"Thank you for your help so far, but what I need is for you to leave." I said it as gently and as calmly as I could. I didn't want to hurt him, but the longer he stayed, the harder it would be to move forward without him.

He tensed, seemingly on the verge of arguing with me. In the end, his shoulders slumped and his gaze locked on mine.

"You know where I'll be if you change your mind."

I did. He would be watching. Always watching. Almost a thousand years, and never had we found a way for me to call him from the afterlife, but I knew as sure as I had bones in my body that if I needed him he would be there.

My eyes never left his as the white mist surrounded him, and then he was gone, leaving me to sort my shit out for myself.

30

Katerina

MAGIC TRICKLED THROUGH my limbs, as sluggish as tree sap. I'd expended the bulk of my power in the first twenty minutes of practice, and already I pulled on my reserves. I longed for the days when I could battle for hours without fatigue. That was the kind of stamina I needed for what was coming, but it would take a miracle to train my way back in the time we had.

In the old days, I would have sparred with Emrick. His years as a sorcerer were long behind him, but he understood my magic in a way no one else in this modern world could. More than that, he could take my hits without injury, which was ideal. Killing my allies during training sessions was not the best way to win a battle.

Instead, I was left fighting air, summoning fireballs and hurling them into the wide expanse of the frosty lake.

I jumped from fire to ice, releasing my heat only to absorb it, attempting to cool the air around me. My reach wasn't as far as it used to be, and only with direct contact could I create layers of ice with any speed or ease, but the magic moved more smoothly than it had a few days ago.

"You still think you can beat Mikhail with force alone?"

I looked up to find Barrett leaning against a tree trunk, a black-garbed smear against the snowy backdrop. He stood with his arms crossed, his expression blank, one foot over the other.

If Emrick reminded me of a panther, Barrett was a basilisk—quick, ready to strike, and with the stony stare to boot.

But if he was trying to intimidate me, he didn't succeed.

"No." I drew more fire into my hands. "But I do think I'll stand a better chance of staying conscious if I stretch first. Unless you're against practice as a rule? You don't run drills between battles, just grab your weapons and hope for the best?"

The muscles that padded every inch of his body argued otherwise, but they also made him a very large, very easy target to vent my frustration on.

"Regular practice is smart," he said. "Trying to binge-practice before battle is a sure way to burn out."

He wasn't wrong.

I threw the flames over the lake, releasing them so they spread out in a wide net and hit the water in a row of sizzles. "We don't have time for you to be right."

"We don't know how much time we have."

"His test run succeeded. He won't drag his feet. We need to find that warehouse and stake it out. Cameras, sentries, whatever we can get. If he waits longer than a week, I'd be surprised."

I scraped the dregs of my magic, held out my hands, and breathed to find stillness. Which did not come easily with James "Judgey" Barrett standing behind me. When I finally found it, I extended my senses to grasp the water in the winter air. My power fought against me, but I relaxed into the lap of it in my veins and gently pushed it outwards.

When I opened my eyes again, I smiled to find snow falling in patterns around my head.

How long had it been since I'd played with that trick?

"I've already messaged Tony," Barrett said, sounding completely unimpressed by my little demonstration. Not that I expected anything else. Santa could pop out of the snowbank beside me, and Barrett would ask why he was shirking his responsibilities by leaving the North Pole.

"Does Tony have any ideas about this place Rhys Saw?" I asked.

"He's been updating me, says he's narrowed it down to a few possibilities. We should have something by end of day."

I sank deeper into my magic, once again trying to find the stillness in the air. The dryness. The static. Fire was my primary skill, ice a handy second, but once upon a time there had been a third. My ability to wield lightning had come to me later, a delightful surprise after centuries of believing the talent had died with my father.

Emrick had taught me how to reach it. His words of advice still pulsed in my ears so many hundreds of years later. But the sparks had never come easily for me, and as my powers had receded, my mastery over lightning had been the first to disappear.

When I couldn't connect with it, I set it aside. I didn't have time to waste on rusted magic. Better to hone my strengths.

I reversed my energy again, pushing heat down my arms and spreading fire between my palms until it formed a wide band. When I pulled my hands apart, the band stretched and thinned. Not anywhere close to the whip I'd once been able to make, but I could work with this in a pinch. I released the fire and sent it over the water. The flames pooled on either end of the band and formed a bolus that flipped one end over the other until it hit the surface of the lake.

"Huh," I said. "That's new."

Still no reaction from the statue behind me.

I reached for my magic again, but this time it wheezed in my blood, dragging my energy with it, and I dropped my hands to my sides. My heart raced and my head throbbed. I didn't want to stop, but Barrett was right. If I kept pushing, I would burn out and be useless until I recovered.

Frustrated, I headed back to the house.

"What about Rhys?" Barrett asked, falling into step beside me.

"What about him?"

"He's an asset. Will you bring him with us?"

I jerked to a halt, one foot on the back patio, and turned to stare at him. "Are you seriously asking if I'm going to bring an eighteen-year-old non-magical to a fight against a hundred power-hungry witches? No, Barrett. The answer is no."

"We can use him, Kat. Right now, we can't afford to be choosy."

"And I can't afford to lose my—Maera's son in an effort to clean up my mess. After all your lectures about running in without a plan, you don't think dragging an untrained teenager into battle constitutes rash and unthinking?"

"I think we need to accept we're outmatched. We need every resource we can pull."

"If only there was an organization that swore to do their part in keeping magic users in line."

Barrett's gaze drifted to the right. "Tony's asked his superiors for an assessment of their team after what happened last time. Their field agents are on lockdown until they confirm there's no leak."

I pressed my lips together. "Again I need to ask—what good are these people?"

He scowled. "At least they're around, which is more than you've been for the past fifty years."

"Yeah, look at them go."

I shook my head and pushed my way into the house. Barrett stuck close behind me. It was only four-thirty, but already Maera had dinner simmering on the stove. The sun had almost set, and the sky was dark with incoming snow clouds.

A belated shiver ran through me as the warmth of the kitchen hugged my chilled limbs, and I stared longingly at the couch, ready to drop into it and take a nap.

Instead, I hauled myself to the kitchen table. Fatigue tugged at my concentration, but I didn't have time to give in to it. Not until we had a solid plan in front of us.

"We should head to Toronto first thing tomorrow," I said.

Barrett leaned against the kitchen counter and crossed his arms. "To be closer when Tony gets back to us?"

"You're assuming the warehouse Rhys Saw is in or near Toronto?" Maera asked as she slid a tray of potatoes into the oven to roast.

"I am," I said. "He'll have to pull so many witches from outlying areas that keeping the meeting place central increases his odds of a full house. There are also enough empty warehouses lying around that he'll be confident about covering his tracks."

Barrett's phone buzzed. He pulled it out of his pocket and pushed off from the counter to take the seat next to me. "It's Tony. He says he thinks he found the warehouse." He didn't take his eyes off the screen while he waited for the next message. *Buzz.* "A place outside Oakville." Another buzz, and his eyes narrowed. "He has a good idea about timeframe as well thanks to the fireworks Rhys thought he heard."

That piqued my interest. I hadn't been certain the loud pops were significant. This was why I kept Maera around; she tended to be much more detail-oriented than I was.

Buzz. "A few blocks away from the likely location, there's a grand reopening for a fancy club coming up."

"Fancy enough for fireworks?" When he nodded, I asked, "When?"

His phone stayed silent. We stayed silent. The tension in the room built.

Maera left her cooking to stand at my shoulder. Barrett stared at his phone.

Buzz.

Barrett's shoulders tensed, and I managed to cling to my patience for the few agonizing seconds it took him to process whatever he'd read. Which I guessed was bad news.

"Three days from now," he finally said.

I forced out a breath. All right. Three days. Better than I'd expected, really. Three days to scrub off a few decades of dusty magic. Seventy-two hours for us to come up with a strategy on how to kick Mikhail's ass. Totally doable.

My stomach twisted into knots.

We were so screwed.

As though the universe knew I needed to hit pause on my spinning thoughts, a knock sounded at the door. Maera left my side to answer it, but I stood up and caught her arm. "I think your meat is overcooking."

She raised an eyebrow in silent contradiction but veered towards the stove, and I took the door.

When I pulled it open, my brain stuttered and my jaw dropped. "Adrian?"

It was now five o'clock and the sun had set, but he would have left his house around noon. He'd taken a huge risk to come visit.

My friend grinned, flashing his fangs, and stepped into the house. His brown eyes were ringed with dark crimson, and I hoped Barrett was up for some cuddle time. This vampire was hungry.

"What are you doing here?" I looked down the driveway to watch a limo with dark-tinted windows back up and drive away. Adrian didn't drive and Barrett was here, so he'd had to rent a driver for the afternoon. He must have known I needed some good counsel. My smile cut short as the answer clued in. "Emrick went to see you, didn't he?"

Adrian chuckled and pulled me in for a hug. "Yes, tesoro, he did. He told me what he found in that warehouse and that you might need me. You can be angry with him or you can be pleased to see me. Unfortunately, you can't be both."

"I might have called you," I pointed out. Adrian responded with a subtle raising of his perfect eyebrow, and I huffed. "In this case, I would have. I confess, I need help."

I hated asking for help from most people. Adrian and Emrick had always been my exceptions, but I'd been trying to respect Adrian's retirement. None of us could have expected this turn of events.

Though in this world where history had a bad habit of repeating itself, maybe we should have.

Adrian kept his arm around me. "Walk with me, Katerina."

He detoured quickly to give Maera a kiss in greeting, and she beamed at him. Her hands fidgeted on the counter, every move revealing her wish to make him something to eat. Alas, her love language was barred by his vampiric digestive system.

Barrett rose from his chair, and Adrian paused long enough to set his hand on his thrall's shoulder. "I won't be long."

Barrett nodded and sat down, then I led Adrian downstairs and out the back door into the frigid evening air.

"Now," my friend began as we moved away from the house, through the trees, down the snowy beach, "tell me everything Emrick wouldn't have."

I ran him through the entire disastrous mission thus far, from the masquerade—leaving out my dance with Emrick—the fight at Rune the Day, the battle in the warehouse, and Rhys's latest visions.

"I don't think I've felt this outmatched since some of our first hunts." I crossed my arms against the chill and stared out over the water. In the distance, snow had begun to fall, obscuring the lake and moving closer. The frosted wind teased my hair where it had slipped free of my braid.

Adrian tucked a loose strand behind my ear. "Remember the hags in Prague?"

I scowled. "There were three of them. But thank you for bringing it up."

That had been a nasty hunt. I'd found bits of carcass in my hair for weeks afterwards.

Adrian chuckled. "I'm just saying, this is not your first challenge, cuore mio. You're stuck because Mikhail has been a thorn in your paw for decades. You've let him get into your head."

"I wish that's all this was. That patron of his worries me." I tilted my head to look at him. "Any news there?"

A crease deepened across his forehead. "Nothing. Whoever it is has kept a low profile. I'd guess a high-level witch. Someone from the Raisers, perhaps?"

The Death Raisers was a coven of dark witches. I'd eradicated them more than once, but they were like cockroaches. Gross, difficult to kill, and evidence of a greater problem.

"It's a good place to start. Maybe I'll get lucky and when I track down Mikhail, this other person will be there, too. Two pains in my ass with one fireball."

Adrian smirked. "As the old saying goes."

We stood in silence for a while, drinking in the wind, watching the darkening sky.

"I don't know how to beat him on my own." The words were out before I knew what I was going to say, but once I'd said them, I appreciated how lost and defeated I felt.

Adrian turned to face me and took my hands. "By finding yourself."

I kept my head down, focused on the smoothness of his skin, the comfort of his cool touch.

"You've been lost for a long time, tesoro." His voice was gentle but left no room for argument. "Long before you and Emrick parted ways. You've floundered in the everyday routine of your life and gotten trapped in it."

A lump formed in my throat, and tears pricked the corners of my eyes. I didn't want to face this truth. Not ever, but especially not now on top of everything else.

Adrian released one hand to set the crook of his finger under my chin. Reluctantly, I raised my gaze to his. "Am I wrong?"

"No." It came out as a whisper, and he kissed my forehead.

"There's no shame in needing a rest, Katerina. Immortality is a burden more often than it is a blessing. But you can't keep hiding. If the promise you made to your family no longer fuels you, perhaps it's time to consider a new purpose."

I grunted through my tears. "Now you sound like Maera."

"She comes from a line of very wise women," he said. He would know considering he'd been the one to hire Maera's grandmother to work for me. He'd known their family as well and as long as I had.

He pulled back and met my eye again. "If you want to overpower Mikhail, your motivations, your desires, your *will* need to be stronger than his, and the only way to ensure that is to decide why it matters that you win. You need to rediscover your drive, the force that made you walk out of Palonia and, instead of burying yourself in misery as you might have done, strive to dominate the magical world. If you can do that, if you can remember who you are, Katerina of Palonia, you'll defeat him. Without question."

31

Katerina

ADRIAN HEADED INSIDE to enjoy his dinner with Barrett, but I remained where I was.

The clouds had moved closer, snowflakes drifting on the wind to caress my cheeks and dress up my hair. They danced and teased and distracted my thoughts from everything Adrian had said.

Until, finally, I was ready to close my eyes and let go of everything I'd been hiding behind.

For so long, I'd run away from my pain, not wanting to feel how deeply it burrowed. It mixed with my blood, pumped through my muscles, as much a part of my life force as the air I breathed.

Tonight, pushed by my friend's counsel and the seemingly impossible task ahead of me, by my confusion over Emrick and my fears for Rhys, I leaned into it.

I pictured my family the way they were that fateful night. Not afterwards, when my life had been torn apart, but before the ritual. The laughter and dancing. The love and kindness and cooperation that had been a mainstay of life in Palonia.

There had been challenges enough, petty dramas and squabbles, but through it all, we'd had each other. In that community, I had been taught to defend what mattered most—our family, our home.

In the eyes of that community, I'd been a disappointment. Unable to master my magic, unable to become a useful member of a society whose mission was to keep the world safe from magical threats.

The night of the bonfires, I'd failed my family for the last time.

I wouldn't fail them again. The people inside the house behind me, wrestling their own demons, their own fears, their own pain, were worth fighting for. Even as human as they were. Even as mortal as they were.

The drive to uphold my promise burned through me, and I summoned fire into my palms. My magic had only begun to recover from my earlier practice, but I ignored my exhaustion, the uncomfortable pull in my veins. Two fireballs burned over my hands, and I closed my eyes to sink deeper into my power.

Once upon a time, this small amount of fire had been as much as I was capable of wielding.

Alodie had laughed at me.

My father had tried to walk me through the next steps of how to project the flames in an offensive attack, and my Gran had assured me that even if I never progressed, I was no less a sorceress because of it.

They had died believing this was all I would ever be.

But I'd come a long way since my small village lessons. Since the cruel gazes of three treasonous women had been replaced by a pair of silver eyes with the patience of a thousand years.

With Emrick's help, I'd come into the potential that had stayed hidden inside me for so long. He'd shown me how much I'd stood in my own way, how the weight of expectation had formed a barrier around my power.

Over the years, I'd replaced that barrier with a new one. One made of depression and doubt that my purpose would ever be fulfilled.

It was time to break those shackles.

I may have lost the drive to hunt down rampaging harpies, but destroying the ritual that had stolen my son from me?

Mikhail believed he knew what I was capable of. It was time I proved him wrong.

My magic expanded, spreading past my arms, past my fingertips, and I opened my eyes to watch the fireball burst forth from my hands and hover above the freezing lake. Another, and another.

Once I'd dotted the water with flickering beacons, I let the heat fade and latched on to the water in the dry air. Frost crept over my fingers, and bit by slow bit, ice spikes formed in my palms.

Balancing their weight like well-made daggers, I hurled them towards the beacons. One by one, the fireballs went out, until again I was alone in the darkness.

My heart beat a frantic rhythm against my ribs, and my legs trembled.

A cry built deep in my chest, and I let it loose as I sent a blast of flames like fireworks into the air. A victory cry as I finally, for the first time in so long, felt a part of myself come back to life.

This was who I was. My true self. Not the woman who'd pulled a blanket over her head and attempted to block out the world. Not the woman who ran from the people who'd hurt her and spurned those who tried to help.

I was nothing without my family, and if my flesh and blood couldn't be with me, then maybe it was time to fight for a new one.

All these years, I'd pushed back against getting close to anyone I knew I'd lose. Maera, Rhys—even Barrett. I leaned on them, cared for them, but never grew attached. Adrian was the only family I had. Or so I'd told myself.

But what was family if not the people who faced life's challenges with you, who offered advice and support and gave you a safe place to come home to? Who said family had to be blood—in fact, wasn't it better to choose who you fought alongside, rather than whoever fate and genetics happened to bind you to?

Emrick's silver eyes drifted past my closed eyelids, and I gently swept them away. I would find a way to solve that particular issue, but not yet. For now, I sank into the warmth of the revelation that would save me.

I would have chosen my family in Palonia.

I would choose my family now.

I would fight to protect them.

And I would win.

But not alone.

With my magic pumping through my veins like a drug, I returned to the house.

32

Katerina

WHEN I STEPPED into the warm kitchen, I found Rhys sitting at the table, scrolling his phone and looking despondent.

Maera was still at the counter, having gone from dinner prep to dinner finale as she scooped a heap of cooked carrots onto a plate. By the surreptitious glances she threw at Rhys over her shoulder, she was aware of his low mood.

I dropped into the seat next to him, and as I watched him flip through his social media apps, I considered what Barrett had said earlier.

And what Adrian had said.

And what Maera and Emrick—hell, even Mikhail had said.

Purpose was everything.

Without it, we were drifting along with the clock just waiting for it to stop ticking.

For some of us, that would never happen, and each second would feel like an eternity. For everyone else, it was over so quickly that each tick was a new regret of missed opportunity.

Rhys was untrained. He was young. But he was also stuck between two worlds with no idea how to move forward. The mundane world would reject him for being too strange, and the magical world would kill him if he didn't have the skills to survive.

Who better to teach him than me?

Did I want him going up against Mikhail? Not a chance in all the hells. But Barrett was right; we needed help.

Before I had time to consider our options further, Barrett and Adrian came into the kitchen. Barrett looked relaxed if tired, and the red had vanished from Adrian's eyes.

The vampire took one look at me, and his usual barely-there smile lit up his face. He gave me a nod as he took his place at the table across from me.

Barrett slid into the chair beside him. He glanced at Rhys, then looked at me. "So? What have you decided?"

It was kind of him to assume I'd decided anything. Unless Adrian had shared the details of our conversation during their private time. It wasn't possible Barrett had decided to have faith in me—the world hadn't stopped turning.

I clasped my hands on the table. "I've decided I'm going to give myself up to Mikhail."

Dishes clattered on the counter, Rhys looked up from his phone, and Barrett blinked.

"That's a stupid idea," he said.

"That's very helpful, thank you," I replied, though the retort was mostly habit.

"Kat Palon, what on earth are you saying?" Maera asked as she came over to the table and sank into the chair next to Rhys. Her eyes were wide with horror, but I didn't let myself be drawn into it.

"Care to elaborate?" Adrian asked. Unlike the others, no hint of doubt shadowed his expression. He had full confidence in my as-yet undisclosed idea, and I was determined to earn it.

"All this time, I've been chasing him. He always knows I'm coming, and he's always ready to evade me. During the masquerade, he invited me to join him. I assumed it was to take something from me, and now I see exactly what he was hoping to get. My power at the base of his spell would give him a serious energy boost."

Barrett leaned back in his chair. "You think your power would be a good enough reason for him to let you get close?"

Centuries of repressed anger at the women who'd originally cast this spell slithered up my spine, and I squeezed my hands closed. "This ritual he's attempting needs a lot of fuel to keep the fires lit. For one person, we're looking at a minimum of a hundred witches. Knowing Mikhail, he'll over-estimate to ensure it works. With me among the others, it would guarantee a full tank. Draining my blood will also make it easy for him to lop off my head and get rid of me for good. If he's gunning for immortality, he won't want to look over his shoulder for eternity."

I waited for Barrett's arguments, but to my surprise he kept his mouth shut.

"How will you do it?" Rhys asked. I doubted he was aware of how far he'd leaned over the table, his green eyes bright with interest, his brow creased in concern.

I pulled on a smug smile. "That part I'll leave up to Barrett."

Another blink from the walking statue. "Excuse me?"

"You keep telling me we're partners in this. Well, partner, give me a plan."

Barrett licked his lips and ran his hand over his head. I'd seen him silent often enough, but never speechless.

I was hinging a good chunk of our success on someone who'd always hated me, and I held my breath, curious to learn how badly I'd messed this up.

Then his dark eyes shone, and his posture straightened. "I'm going to need a coffee."

In the end, Barrett needed much more than coffee before he was able to come up with an idea he considered worth sharing. We finished coffee, dinner, an entire blueberry pie, and more coffee by the time he informed us with a few vague grunts that he was ready.

"For the record, I still think your idea is stupid," he began.

"Your opinion has been noted," I assured him.

"But if you're right that he won't try to kill you the moment he sees you...?" He raised his eyebrow to highlight his question.

"He won't. If nothing else, he'll want the show of making me a sacrifice. I'm their tormentor, remember? Getting rid of me would be community service, which can only help his reputation. He has a lot to prove to these people so they don't turn on him the moment they realize something's wrong."

Barrett nodded and continued, "Then we have a few options. The first step will be confirming Tony's found the right warehouse. Still no word from him, but I've followed up. Once that's done, I agree with what you said earlier. We stake the place out and get familiar with the area. Tony's people can't go in with us, but maybe they can help us with the prep work."

"I don't want them knowing our plan," I said. "Not all of it, anyway. We've asked them to search for the warehouse, and it'll look suspicious if we ask them to stop, but if they have a leak, we'll be destroying our chances before we make our first move." I tapped my fingers against the table. "What about setting up wards around the area to keep the witches contained? I don't want Mikhail running if we finally pin him down."

I considered my options, but again, only one name came to mind. I texted Poppy, then set my phone aside.

"Even without magic, we can lay a few traps of our own," Barrett said, "but the key will be getting you to Mikhail so you can cut the ritual off at the head."

"*Before* he starts the spell," I added. "On that note, I want it to be clear right now, in front of everyone—if the ritual starts, you need to keep your distance. Stay out of the warehouse, keep to the perimeter. Don't drink anything, don't listen to the chanting. Your job will be to deal with the witches once they scatter. Got it?"

Barrett looked to Adrian as though asking for permission, and Adrian's gaze locked on mine, first searching then accepting. He dropped his chin in a nod. "Very well. James, you heard her. If the ritual begins, you stay away."

Barrett scowled, and I appreciated his reticence. I knew his frustration stemmed from his desire to tear Mikhail's head off and not from any concern for me, but I appreciated it nonetheless.

"May I offer my suggestions now?" I asked.

He nodded, and I caught a hint of Adrian's smirk before he hid it behind his hand.

"We fucked up royally by going in together last time," I said. "We missed the traps, allowed ourselves to be surrounded, and weren't prepared to fight our way out. Lesson learned and all that. We know they'll be expecting you somewhere, but we can use your position to our advantage. We can make them think there's more than just you out there."

Barrett cocked his head in thought. "Do you think the necromancer would be willing to help?"

I glanced at the series of unanswered texts to Poppy's number. "She's gone AWOL, so I'm going to say no."

Something I'd deal with later.

"What about you?" I asked Adrian. "Any interest in joining the team?"

He pulled his lips back to bare his fangs. "You know I'll always support you, tesoro, but I think it would be wiser for me to sit this one out. What with blood magic and necromancers being involved."

Adrian, being an undead blood drinker, would be vulnerable to both.

Disappointing but valid.

"I can do it," Rhys said.

Maera sucked in a breath, and her face paled, but she said nothing. I suspected she couldn't have spoken if she'd wanted to.

A refusal sat on my lips, ready to make the leap into the room, but the sounds wouldn't come.

Again that word echoed through my head. *Purpose.* I didn't want him there, couldn't bear the thought of our plan going wrong and him getting hurt, but I couldn't turn him down.

Maera recovered and crossed her arms. "That's not happening."

Rhys looked to me to argue on his behalf, but it was Adrian who spoke. "I know you're worried for him, Maera, but perhaps Rhys will prove to be the turning point we need to win this."

"No. I'm not having it."

"Mum, I promise, I'll be—"

"Don't promise you'll be careful, because you can't promise that. You have no idea what you're walking into."

"I know it'll be a fight."

"And how many fights have you been in before, hmm? At what point did you spend years learning how to defend yourself? I'm sorry, Rhys, but no. You'd be an untested child going up against a bloodthirsty criminal."

Rhys bristled. "I'm not—"

"You're *my* child, Rhys Byrne. You don't get to argue that one with me."

He frowned, his fair eyebrows drawing down to set off the furious green glimmer in his eyes. "Mum, I know what happens in that room if this hunt fails. The image of it has haunted me since my first vision. If I can stop it from happening, then I need to help."

Mother and son waged a silent war. My heart thrummed in my chest, uncertain of who I wanted to come out victorious. Every time I decided on Maera, I thought of Rhys's expression when he'd been unable to work out the details of his last vision. I hated that he believed he wasn't good enough because he hadn't found his place in the world.

Finally, Maera's shoulders slumped. She pressed her fingers into her eyes and cleared her throat, and when she dropped her hands, tears lingered on her cheeks.

When she met my eye, her gaze was hard as flint.

"You make sure my boy comes home, Katerina Palon. Promise me."

I nodded, and the weight of my promise settled in my soul. Whatever else happened, however else this played out, I would not break my word.

33

Katerina

BARRETT AND I took the next day to walk Rhys through the fundamentals of combat. In no way, shape, or form would he be ready to walk into that warehouse with us, but he stood a better chance of surviving by the time the sun set than he would have without the practice.

I'd armed him with the remaining potions I'd bought from Poppy, so at the very least he'd be able to protect himself.

Barret had given him one of his knives despite Maera's obvious disapproval, and I crossed my fingers no one got close enough for him to have to use it. Once he'd taken this step into my world, there was no way my sweet protégé would maintain his youthful, mundane innocence, but the last thing I wanted was to see it shattered by him having to kill someone.

I would do my best to take that burden on myself. My soul was scarred enough that a few more deaths wouldn't make much difference.

Around noon, Tony emailed Barrett some satellite images of the warehouse he'd identified as Mikhail's meeting place.

As Rhys scrolled through the images, his face blanched. "This is it. Definitely." He pointed to one of the pictures of the two-storey white-washed building on the edge of Lake Ontario. "I recognize the graffiti on the side here. Something happens by that graffiti. I don't know what, but something."

I rested my hand on his shoulder. "Whatever it is, we'll be ready for it. We wouldn't even know where to go if not for you. We haven't made a single move yet, and you've already saved people."

He smiled, but it was so laced with fear that it pierced my heart. Without thinking, I threw my arms around his neck and squeezed. He hugged me back, and I closed my eyes at the contact.

How long had it been since I'd enjoyed something as simple as a hug?

His arms went slack and fell by his sides, and with reluctance, I let go, figuring I'd overstayed my welcome. But when I pulled away, I took in his white eyes and blank expression.

"What do you see?" I asked.

"You falling. Bleeding. Screaming. On your knees, eyes full of fear. Someone standing over you, knife raised. Circles in the air, on the floor. Pink smoke."

He shuddered and wobbled on his feet, but Barrett was there to catch his elbow and steady him before he fell.

I grabbed a kitchen chair, and Rhys dropped into it, rubbing his face. I knelt beside him. "Are you all right?"

"No?" he said, and his voice sounded small. "I don't want anything to happen to you, Kat. But what I Saw…"

He shivered, and I wrapped my arms around him again. He bowed his head into the crook of my neck, and I stroked my fingers through his hair. "Remember, Rhys, your visions aren't set in stone. We're going in prepared, and with something Mikhail will never expect."

Rhys looked up, his green eyes shadowed. "What's that?"

I winked. "You."

He huffed a laugh. "We all know I won't be much help. But whatever I can do, I will."

I rose to my feet and brushed his hair out of his face. "Your presence will do more than you think. Mikhail believes he can anticipate every move I make. This time, we lead the dance."

The drive back to Toronto was quiet and tense, but not in the same way as the drive home had been. Then, it had been fear for Rhys, frustration at my failure, and concern that I didn't have what it took to stop Mikhail from ruining the lives of thousands, if not more.

Now, I'd cleared my trunks of all that bullshit garbage and was left with a different type of fear—the fear that I'd fail again, that something would happen to Rhys, and that I'd let my family down a second time.

Not different at all, really. That bullshit garbage was tough to shake.

I couldn't afford to let those thoughts get the better of me, but I kept them in full view all the same. They grounded me, reminded me of the dangers ahead. To assume I would win without trouble, without loss, would be as dangerous as believing I'd fail.

We arrived at Adrian's house in Kensington Market by noon, which gave us more than enough time to head to the warehouse to get a feel for the place.

I'd debated the wisdom of letting Rhys come with us, but he wanted to find out if being there in person would clarify any of his visions. Despite my better judgement, I allowed it, and within an hour and a half, we were parked three blocks down from the site of our future battle.

We kept our distance from the building, using Barrett's binoculars and my sensitivity to magic to take in more than what we could see from the road.

On the surface, there wasn't much here except some docks behind the warehouse and a few outbuildings used for extra storage. The nearest neighbour was a kilometre away.

The stockyard outside was covered in snow, but by the tire treads that marked the snowfall with slush, the abandoned building was in regular use.

If we had any doubts we were in the right place, they disappeared when Rhys had to hop out of the car to vomit into a snowbank.

"It's like I can smell the blood," he explained after he cleaned himself up and returned to the back seat.

Barrett and I got out of the car to take a look around.

Before Rhys closed his door, I grabbed a bottle of water from the stakeout bag in the front and passed it to him. "You stay here. Stay low, text me if you see anyone."

The odds of Mikhail not keeping an eye on the place were slim, and I didn't want him knowing about Rhys before he had to.

Or ever, preferably.

Rhys didn't grumble as he sank lower in the seat, protected from any prying eyes by the tinted windows.

Barrett and I maintained a slow pace as we crept along the property's perimeter. He kept an eye out for any physical triggers, while I remained wary of magical ones. Although neither of us stumbled on anything, we knew better than to think we were safe. Mikhail would work on the assumption that we would show up. Our only hope of taking him by surprise was to walk voluntarily into his trap and pack more power than his army did.

"Other than the main doors, the only other way out is along the water," Barrett observed from where we stood almost five hundred metres away from the building.

"It'll be difficult to block that approach. Unless we destroy the dock."

Barrett shifted the binoculars to get a better view of the structure. "Metal. Fire won't do much. But we could target the boat."

"Rhys will have the potions—set him on that. The rear of the building shouldn't be too busy." I frowned at the graffiti along the wall. "Rhys said something happened here. Let's make sure he's prepared so, whatever it is, he survives it. We'll have to make sure the timing is right."

I closed my eyes and extended my senses along the molecules in the air. They pushed back against me, teasing me with their presence, tempting me to play with them, but among all the natural currents, I didn't detect much magic. If there was a ward around the building, it wasn't a strong one.

"They're definitely expecting us." I opened my eyes and crossed my arms.

"Good," Barrett said. I raised an eyebrow, and he shrugged. "It'll be Mikhail's last day on earth. Why not give him a going-away present?"

We returned to the car to find Rhys half-asleep. He hadn't seen anyone or anything while we'd been gone, and the visions of the past couple days were catching up with him.

Barrett took us back to Adrian's place. Rhys collapsed on the couch and fell asleep, Barrett disappeared into the gym in the basement, and I headed up to my room.

I had my own training to do.

While I had the time and space to myself, I sat cross-legged on my bed and slipped into a deep meditation. With every inhale and exhale, I sank deeper into my magic, allowing it to flow through me, in and out like the tide. With every flex of power, I imagined it getting stronger, more limber, and ready to respond when summoned.

I would be relying heavily on it in the fight to come, a terrifying prospect when there was so much room for everything to go wrong.

I'd have a few of Poppy's potions along with me, but if even part of our plan went well, I wouldn't have them for long.

My stomach sloshed with nerves. I would have felt much more confident with Emrick or Adrian by my side, but at the thought, I straightened my spine and raised my chin.

I was strong enough without them. If I didn't believe that, then what was I doing?

With Emrick in mind, I opened my eyes to scan the shadows of my room, searching for him in every corner. Nothing. He was keeping his promise to me, and I had to be grateful. Even if a not-small part of me wished he'd break his word.

Stressed, exhausted, apprehensive about tomorrow, I stripped down and crawled under the covers. What I needed was a solid night's sleep. Tomorrow we'd find out just how much of my old self still existed.

I rose with the midday sun, stretched, and dressed in my usual hunting garb of black leather pants, black T-shirt, runed gloves.

The rest of the day passed in a blur. Barrett spent most of his time in the gym, Rhys in the bathroom, and me doing everything I could to prime my magic without accidentally setting fire to the living room.

By the time the sun began to set, my nerves were frayed and ready to snap if we didn't get moving soon.

I'd never come as close to kissing Barrett as when he grabbed his keys and ushered us out the door. He and Rhys were both dressed in black, and Rhys had pulled a black tuque over his bright red hair. Against the snow, we would all stand out, but at least the poor guy wouldn't be a glaring beacon in the darkness.

Rhys's face was pale, his lips pressed firmly together, but I was impressed when he managed to keep his stomach the entire drive to Oakville.

Barrett, of course, seemed as relaxed as if we were heading to the grocery store.

Maybe more so. Grocery stores were stressful, unpleasant places.

As for me, my anxieties settled the closer we got to the warehouse.

I knew what we were up against, both in terms of the threat and what we stood to lose if we didn't stop Mikhail from completing his ritual.

Barrett parked where he had yesterday, and the three of us piled out of the car. We didn't speak. There was nothing else to say. We'd gone through the plan a dozen times on the drive here; we all knew where we needed to be and what needed to be done.

The guys faded into the shadows that would take them along the perimeter of the property, while I started towards the front doors. Poppy had never gotten back to me, so we were moving in without wards, but as long as Barrett, Rhys, and I kept the fight contained, we would make do.

The satchel draped across my body hung light at my waist, and I kept my hand on it to keep it from bouncing against my hip. Rhys had taken most of the potions, but a few were tucked inside. With luck, I'd get a chance to use them before they were taken from me. While my magic was humming happily in my blood, it was weak, and I didn't want to drain myself before I needed it.

My footfalls fell silently on the snow, and no other sounds broke through the quiet night. Soon enough, the fireworks display would begin and their thunderous booms would drown out anything that happened here, but for now there was me, the snow... and the murmured voices of people trying to creep up on me.

I swallowed a sigh. Points to them for trying, I supposed.

Three figures stepped into view. They'd travelled behind the trees that lined the property, and as soon as they stepped into the open, potions were in their hands. I readied some of my own and hurled them with all my strength. One of my vials smashed into one of theirs mid-flight, and the spells mixed together to form a burst of icy fire that struck the ground and both melted the snow and froze the water.

One of the witches had opted to run towards me and now tried to back-peddle. Their foot slipped on the ice, and they face-planted in the flames. Their screams tore through my ears, but I didn't have time to block them out before a second witch threw another vial. I sidestepped it as it cracked against the ice. Green fog rose from the shattered glass, and I held my breath as I danced out of range and threw a vial at the third witch still standing among the trees.

They raised a hand and shouted an incantation. A ward formed in the air and blocked the magic from the potion before it struck them.

Neat trick. These witches had leveled up.

I turned my back on them and fled towards the warehouse. Their shouts followed me as they rushed to catch up, and another vial smashed at my heels. The potion sprayed the backs of my legs, but the leather kept the worst of the effects off me.

More figures charged from both sides of the building, and I dodged the first two as I threw more vials at them. A blue cloud rose around them, and they dropped into the snow with heaving sobs, as though I'd just killed their beloved pet. An emotion-manipulating spell.

Unfortunately, my interest in the potion's effects distracted me, and I missed the vial coming in on my left. It struck the side of my face, and glass splintered across my cheek. The spell sank into my pores, and I screamed as the burn spread down my neck and up into my skull. It felt as though a million bees were stinging their way through my bloodstream, and I dropped to my knees, unable to see for the pain.

"Grab her!" one of the witches called.

"You grab her—I don't want to get set on fire," another one shot back.

I hissed through my teeth and breathed through the agony as it abated. In another few seconds, my healing ability would have absorbed the magic and I'd be fine. These fools were wasting time.

With a groan, I pushed myself back to my feet and staggered as my head swam. I reached for another vial, but a heavy weight knocked me to the ground. The satchel was torn from my shoulder, and I was unceremoniously rolled onto my stomach, my face pushed into the snow.

Two people grabbed my arms and hauled me up between them.

"Come on, quit dicking around. The high priest wants her for his spell."

I allowed myself to go limp, and one of the people holding me grunted as they rushed to adjust their grip on my arm.

"Drag her if you have to. Mikhail didn't say he needs her conscious."

They jerked me across the ground, wet slush seeping into the tops of my boots, and through the doorway into the warehouse.

The sight of over two hundred witches greeted me, and my mouth went dry. We'd known the numbers would be high, but it was another thing to see it.

Power thrummed in my veins, begging me to release it, but I kept it in check. If I unleashed it here, there was no way I would win on my own against so many without blasting the entire building and killing everyone inside. Possibly myself included.

The witches, all robed and standing, turned to face me, stepping to the side to reveal the man at the top of the circle. He stood in front of a large bubbling pot, a fire built up underneath it to warm the concoction within. I spotted the cups already circulating among the crowd.

Those who'd drunk from it had signed their death warrants, and they had no idea. They wouldn't know until the effects of the ritual kicked in, and until that moment they would fight with everything they had.

And here I was with only my magic to protect me.

The witches who'd dragged me in threw me to the floor. As Mikhail pushed his hood back and graced me with his wild smile and dark, dancing eyes, I could only pray I hadn't made a horrible mistake.

34

Katerina

"KAT PALON," MIKHAIL greeted me, projecting his voice to carry across the room. "I'm so happy you made it in time for the festivities. You were such a wonderful dance partner. I hope you'll give me another turn."

The line was so pompous I couldn't hold back my laugh.

"I don't know if my toes can take the pressure. You're a bit heavy-footed for a waltz."

His smile turned dangerous. "Then I suppose it's best if I stay off the dance floor. Believe me, my plans for the rest of the evening don't require a soft touch."

"I have no doubt about that."

A hooded, hunched witch with a rolling gait left Mikhail's side and shoved a cup in my face. A floral scent followed them, again tantalizing me with its familiarity. Mikhail's patron. I strained to catch a glimpse of their face, but the hood was pulled too low. The hands holding the cup, though, were wrinkled, chalky in colour, and distinctly female.

Mikhail smirked. "Care for a drink?"

"I'll pass, thanks."

One of the witches holding me wrapped my hair in their grip and jerked my head back. It took every effort not to throw my fist in the bastard's face. The hunched figure snagged my chin in her free hand and poured the contents over my mouth. I pressed my lips together, and a third witch stepped in to pinch my nose shut.

I resisted their efforts until my lungs screamed. Lack of oxygen wouldn't kill me, but I couldn't afford to lose consciousness. Not with Barrett and Rhys outside.

With a gasp, I opened my mouth, and the foul liquid spilled down my throat. The putrid flavour dragged me through history to the night of the bonfires, and I retched onto the floor.

The damage had been done, however. All it took was a sip. That potion was once more swimming through my bloodstream, setting me up as one more sacrifice for Mikhail's shift to immortality.

I collapsed onto my hands and breathed through my mouth until my stomach settled, overpowered by memories and horror. Mikhail's rumbling laughter floated around me, stabbing my eardrums, and rage settled in my gut alongside the rancid punch.

The witch with the cup returned to Mikhail's side, and I caught a glimpse of a cruel smile beneath her hood.

"And so we begin," he said. "I want you to know before we start that I've enjoyed your chase, sorceress. Nothing makes a person feel more powerful than knowing someone wants them dead."

A series of replies bubbled on my tongue, but I bit them back. I didn't need to utter a syllable to have the last word. It would be obvious who claimed it soon enough.

Shrugging off the last of my nausea, I summoned my magic into my hands.

Mikhail stood on his own, distracted by his spell, and his followers were staring at him with the eager, dazed expressions of loyal puppies. This was my chance to take him down.

Power surged through me, enveloped me, and by the time I got to my feet, fire swept up my arms and hugged my gloves. I remembered my practice on the beach, the fiery bolus I'd flung over the water.

Flames spread before me, causing sweat to burst through my pores, and I launched them at Mikhail.

Streams of crackling magic soared through the air, two linked fireballs that would cut through anything in its path.

Mikhail and his followers registered my actions a second too late, and the hum of success buzzed through me.

Until the flames bounced off an invisible ward and swept back towards me.

I threw myself to the ground, and the fire caught the witches that had dragged me inside. Their screams filled the warehouse—the horn blast that began the battle.

Mikhail laughed. "You didn't think I'd be so unprepared, did you?"

Dread weighed down my heart. He had a ward of manipulated air? Sorcerer's magic. It would have taken a significant amount of power and time to create, but once again he'd been ready for me.

Or was it the hunched witch?

I didn't have time to get a closer look at them before every other witch reached into their satchels or uttered their incantations, and over a hundred spells flew my way. I pumped my magic into my hands and spun on my feet as I released it in a wall of fire that consumed everything coming at me. Vials smashed against the floor, and more screams sounded as potions missed their mark or my fire got too close.

Beyond the shouts, a baritone voice reciting an incantation vibrated in my ears. Mikhail had begun the ritual.

Everything I'd fought to prevent was coming to pass. Urgency drove me to channel more magic into my hands. Unless I interrupted him, we had about five minutes before the effects of the spell kicked in.

The only silver lining was that just as I'd missed my opportunity, Mikhail had missed his to get rid of me easily. He needed his minions to catch me, but he also needed their blood for his ritual. As long as he stayed focused on the latter, I had a chance of finding another opening to destroy him.

A tiny voice in the back of my head urged me to burn the building to the ground and take everyone out. The witches, Mikhail—myself if I had to. But if I killed us all, how would that make me any better than Mikhail?

I also didn't know if I had enough magic to do it in one fell swoop. Not with so many witches ready to fight back.

I crossed my fingers Rhys and Barrett kept their distance like they were supposed to. Away from the noxious potion, away from having their blood spilled, they would be free to get word to the witch hunters if I fell. I didn't like or trust Tony, but the hunters might be the world's last shot at stopping Mikhail.

More spells flew at me, and I dropped into a crouch as they whizzed over my head. A spell circle glowed in the air, and I summoned my fire and threw it at the circle just before it unleashed. My ears popped, and I was thrown off my feet at the energy pulse. At least ten other witches came with me, and we fell in a heap with me in the middle. Something sharp—a goddamned knife—drove into my side, and I responded with a blast of fire that caught the witches' robes. They rolled away from me, and I tugged the knife free, keeping the hilt in my grip for anyone else who got too close.

My vision wavered, but I summoned more power. Whoever thought a blade to the kidney would kill me hadn't been paying attention.

Reversing my heat, I cooled the air around me, drawing more energy into myself until my blood simmered and a layer of frost covered the floor five metres around where I stood. Unprepared witches slipped and fell as they made their way towards me. The echo of chattering teeth battled

Mikhail's rising voice, and I spotted more than one witch huddled over themselves to stay warm.

Despite my desire to switch back to fire and roast these people for being pains in my ass, I absorbed more heat and watched the frost on the floor thicken into a layer of ice. Not only would the cold help keep everyone off me, but it would slow the effects of the ritual. My cowardice so many years ago had taught me that much.

As I released my power, I made my way through the room, gaining the ground I'd lost thanks to that spell circle. Vials flew at me, but as soon as they came within the sphere of my temperature drop, the glass froze and shattered, raining potions of all sorts over the witches unlucky enough to be in the way.

My side shrieked with every step, and as my body temperature rose with all the heat I absorbed, my consciousness began slipping away. I did my best to fight through the haze, but when I summoned ice spikes into my hands and launched them at Mikhail, my aim was so far off I couldn't begrudge him the smug grin he threw my way.

What I needed was to get these witches running. If I made them scatter, Barrett could start picking them off and clear the way for me to launch another attack at Mikhail. His—or his patron's—wards wouldn't hold forever.

Bangs and bursts reached me from beyond the doors. The fireworks had started. Soon, Rhys would start throwing potions at the boat to box the witches in.

Did I need these witches to die? No. In fact, they were more than welcome to see themselves out. But as long as they were determined to fight me, I wouldn't hold back.

A vial flew over my head, and I dropped to my knee. Agony so intense I saw white slashed through my side at the jarring impact, and I pressed my hand against the knife wound. In a few more minutes, it would start to heal. I just had to hang on that long.

I breathed through the pain as more of the room froze. All around me, people tottered and slipped, crashed into others, or wound up stuck to the ground, tugging desperately at their legs to free their feet from the ice.

A spot on my arm tingled, itched, burned, and I curled my hands into fists to stop myself from scratching. Mikhail's incantation droned on, the pace of it speeding up, the power behind it creating currents of magic in the air. I looked around and watched as the effects of the spell kicked in. So far no horror filled the witches' eyes, no confusion marred their expressions as they fought to take me down.

It would happen soon enough.

We were down to three minutes, if we were lucky, before the itch became so unbearable they tore themselves to pieces for a moment's relief.

I had to get to Mikhail, and these bastards were in my way.

My legs trembled as I pushed myself to my feet.

Heart racing, sweat dripping down my face, I drew in all the heat I'd sucked out of the room and summoned it like streams of fire into my palms. The frozen floor threatened to take me out, but it was my ice, and I walked as though I owned it.

A woman ran towards me, slipped, caught herself, and threw a spell that zipped past my head, only just missing the side of my face. The reek of singed hair filled my nostrils, and I returned her spell with a fireball. She dodged the flames, and they struck a man behind her who'd been about to reach into his satchel to pull out a vial of his own.

The woman made to grab another spell, but a gunshot sounded behind me, and the witch dropped to one knee as blood sprayed from her leg.

My eye twitched as I realized Barrett had broken my one rule—to keep his goddamned distance.

I searched the crowd and found him near the doors, weapon raised, blood streaming from a cut on his forehead. Rhys was nowhere to be seen.

I was so wrapped up in glaring at him, I almost missed a spell flying towards my head. The bright flash of a green vial caught the light a moment before it hit me, and I raised my arm to catch it on my glove instead of my face. The glass smashed, the liquid spattered, and smoke rose in tiny tendrils where the droplets ate through my shirt.

I turned to see who had thrown it and spotted a man rushing to replace the weapon he'd launched. Aiming for the crates behind him, I threw a fireball, and the pine slats caught and spread as though they'd been doused with kerosene. The witch tore away from the burst of flame that licked towards him and caught the edges of his robe.

Finally, I reached the middle of the circle. An influx of witches scrambled to stop me, but the projectiles stopped flying the closer I got to Mikhail. Wards or not, they were too worried about hitting him instead of me. In a last-ditch effort, they switched to physical attacks, but my fire kept them at a distance, and Barrett soon drew more of them away.

Tempted as I was to tear them all down, I focused my attention on Mikhail. His followers were gnats buzzing in my ear. He was the wasp's nest.

My skin itched, my body ached, my head spun, but I pushed through the discomfort. As miserable as I was, I'd suffered worse—and Mikhail would experience every ounce of my agony before the end.

He spoke faster, determined to reach the end of the spell, but his dark eyes sparked with fury that a room full of witches hadn't been enough to stop me. Smoke from the cauldron curled towards the ceiling, and the already stifling room grew warmer as the fire around the crates spread.

I threw my stolen knife and grinned when the blade missed him by an inch. At some point in the chaos, his wards had dropped, and his patron was nowhere to be seen. This fight was down to him and me, and the window was closing. He had to know he was finished.

I channelled more fire into my palms and released it with enough force that the flame came out in a wave. It caught the potion bubbling in the pot, and an acidic stench burst forth that made my eyes water and forced Mikhail to retreat. His chant fell silent, his concentration broken, and a thrill of victory ran through me as I prepared to launch myself at him.

I expected him to be furious that I'd destroyed part of his spell and interrupted the other, but his face split into an obnoxious grin, and my blood chilled as I realized too late what I'd done.

Barrett had been safe from the effects of the ritual, but as soon as he inhaled the smoke now pouring from the cauldron and rapidly filling the room, he would be as doomed as everyone else, whether he'd sipped from the cup or not.

A laugh spilled from between Mikhail's lips, and his dark eyes sparkled with glee. My hatred for him ignited the embers within me, and I spat another wave of fire at him, pushing him farther back. He murmured something under his breath, and in the air, a spell circle formed. I stumbled, amazed by the strength of the magic vibrating off him, and dove out of the way before the circle released its power and shot forth a burst of shock waves that tore through the mob behind where I'd stood. A scream pierced my ears, quickly cut short, and I looked over my shoulder to find a fresh corpse on the ground missing the middle of her torso. Behind her, the thick wall of the warehouse was dented.

For a breath, I couldn't move, stunned by Mikhail's power.

He was a witch. He couldn't be anything more than a witch. Yet his spell had carried more weight than anything I'd encountered in the past three hundred years. Just like the ward, it was the sort of air manipulation the sorcerer communities had mastered before they'd died out. Had the patron who'd taught him the immortality ritual also taught him a way to use witchcraft to emulate the sorcery of old?

Fear held me bound.

Even with my renewed motivation, even with my rediscovered magic, I didn't have what it took to overpower this witch. There was no way I could get out of here, surrounded as I was on all sides. Injured. Itching and breathing in the heart of the spell that had changed my life once and now threatened to end it.

Shouts echoed around me and movement caught my eye as the witches opened a path for the rest of their circle. Two witches dragged Rhys forward by his arms. He struggled against them but was unable to gain enough momentum to fight his way free. His tuque was gone, and his red hair stuck out in all directions. His eyes were filled with terror, blood smeared his face, and his satchel was missing. I swallowed a cry, but my heart shattered that he'd been discovered. That I'd broken my promise to Maera—the one promise I'd so wanted to keep.

Beyond him, Barrett was on his knees, a blade at his throat and a dozen witches with a dozen vials arranged in a circle around him.

Mikhail chuckled, and despite the chaos in the room, the sound of his voice carried as he closed the distance between us. He stood over me, lording himself over my loss. The pressure of his superiority bore down on me, and I dropped to my knees.

"What do you think, Ms. Palon? Are you ready to change your mind about that dance?"

35

Katerina

Time stopped.

I wished it had in a literal sense to give me time to slam my fist into Mikhail's nose, slit his throat, and end this farce before he could get out one more conceited syllable. But it was only me, drawing each breath, listening to each racing heartbeat, speeding through all eight hundred-and-seventy-seven years of my life.

Family. Friends. Training. Emrick.

Outrunning Templars. Fighting demons. Escaping war zones.

The years zipped past me in flashes, and I scanned through each one, desperate for the glimmer of a lesson, a memory, a trick I could use to get Barrett, Rhys, and myself out of here.

Mikhail curled his fingers into my hair and tugged my head back to meet his eye. The sharp point of a blade rested against my throat, and I held my breath, not wanting the slightest move to be what took me out of the fight. If he wanted me dead, I would make him work for it.

"When you first came after me forty years ago, I was sure you'd be the end of me. Every time I've come close to greatness, you've been there to get in my way. Not this time, sorceress. This time, you'll help me achieve my goals, and after I'm finished, I'll make sure you never haunt my steps again."

He left the knife where it was and began his incantation from the start. At first, nothing happened, but then the itch that had subsided when the ritual was interrupted set a different fire to my skin.

So much worse than before. It began as a bubbling heat I'd once mistaken as drunkenness and the excitement of the evening. I'd thought my son had rolled in some poison ivy, and my sister had ignored it to shoot glances at the handsome stranger gathering attention on the edges of the crowd.

The heat spread across my body in little pinpricks of pain. Like bug bites I longed to scratch but knew better than to touch.

I wished I could warn Barrett and Rhys to leave them be, but if I spoke, that blade would tear through my flesh before I made it through three words. The madness in Mikhail's smile, the challenge in his eyes to try to stop him, told me as much. The blow wouldn't kill me, but it would incapacitate me, making it all too easy for him to finish the job with his stupid fucking ritual.

Murmurs of confusion and excitement rose through the room as the witches finally noticed the effects of the spell, no longer distracted by keeping me away from their leader. They slapped their arms and scratched their necks. Slowly but surely breaking skin and opening the way for the blood to rise more freely into the air.

Mikhail's smile widened as his voice grew louder, and the itching worsened, now tormenting every inch of my body. The whoops of enthusiasm shifted into cries of concern, and the scratching grew worse. The rustle of fingernails against cloth buffeted my ears like wind in a sail as the movement picked up, and I wanted to clap my hands over my ears to block out the sound.

I squeezed my eyes shut as if that would help and forced myself to stay still, hoping Barrett and Rhys would notice what I was doing and trust me enough to follow my lead.

The thought of them trapped here, caught in this destruction because of my inability to overpower this lone witch, wormed into my brain and warred with my feelings of defeat.

I couldn't give up.

I *wouldn't* give up.

One way or another, I would get them out of this. I was prepared to go down with Mikhail to do it.

I could barely think, the buzzing under my skin too distracting. I needed to shut out the pain, needed a moment of peace to focus. But using the same trick I'd pulled last time wouldn't help me here. Standing so close, Mikhail would know the moment I reversed my heat and cooled my body temperature. At the first hint that I was working against him, he would saw his knife through my neck. This close to victory, he wouldn't allow me to get in his way.

Besides, that trick would only save me.

Just as it had last time.

When I could have done more to save my family. My son.

I could have destroyed Alodie, Mae, and Blythe before they destroyed us, and instead I'd remained huddled against the ground, wrapped in ice to save myself while I waited for the nightmare to be over.

Not today.

Barrett and Rhys needed me to think about more than my own skin.

I considered turning Mikhail into one of Adrian's ice sculptures, but I'd never spread the ice quickly enough—not enough to shut his mouth. No, if I wanted to take him down, I would need more than my basic arsenal.

My heart raced and doubts assailed me, but I tamped them down and did my best to concentrate.

Despite swearing I could do this on my own, I found myself scanning the room for any sight of blond hair and silver eyes, and panic hummed within me when I didn't find them.

I breathed through it. I didn't need Emrick. Anything he had to offer he'd already given me centuries ago. I just had to remember.

Keeping my eyes on Rhys and Barrett to anchor me to the present, I dug past the physical pain and the cold memories of my family. I waded through the years of learning how to tap into my basic elemental magic of fire and ice. They had served me well, but Mikhail had already proved a blast of fire wouldn't be enough to get us out of here. I needed something unexpected.

Deep, deep in the recesses of my mind, the old lessons with Emrick shone like pinpricks of light in the darkness.

Anything is possible for you, Katerina. His voice stroked my mind, that hint of teasing and coaxing. *Once you believe it, once you embrace it, you'll make the world tremble.*

I wondered if he realized how much those words would mean to me almost eight hundred years later. At the time, they'd needled me, made me feel as much of a let-down as my tutors had always believed I was. Because of course Katerina of Palonia couldn't see her own potential. She never could. It was as hidden from her as the sun during a storm.

Time had allowed me to understand what he meant. And how right he'd been.

I'd let that woman doze off over the past century or so, but now it was time to wake her up and remind myself who I'd become with the support of the people who cared about me.

Holding on to Emrick's words, I directed my attention to the energy in the room. Mikhail's growing magic. The blood pulsing out of the veins of those standing nearest me, the droplets moving through the air towards the witch summoning their power. I felt the tug of temptation to grab hold of that power and use it, but the idea repulsed me. I didn't want to win this fight off the backs of others. Not even the witches who had tried so hard to tear me down.

I reached past them and felt the heat of the fire spreading towards us from the edges of the room, the dryness of the air sucking the sweat from my pores and making the itching so much worse.

The roughness of static brushing the edges of my sleeves against my skin.

I stilled.

It had been so long since I'd played with these sparks.

The itch in my side as the knife wound began to knit back together added to the discomfort of the bugs crawling through my veins, the stinging driving me to madness, making me long to scratch through the layers of flesh to ease the agony.

Don't think about it. Just do it.

I squeezed my hands into tight fists and dragged my mind to the stillness. The calm within the chaos. A near impossibility as the screams in the room grew louder, scraping my nerves with their terror and anguish.

I pulled myself back to that memory of so long ago. A peaceful garden on a warm autumn day. Emrick standing behind me, close enough I felt his breath on the back of my neck as he persuaded me I was more than I believed myself to be.

Wrapping his confidence around me like a mantle, I latched on to the static in the air. It tingled over my skin, made my fingers jump, and I nearly lost my hold on it. I squeezed my eyes shut to maintain my control. The electric buzz was uncomfortable after so many years of not experiencing it. Sparks zapped from my fingertips, prevented from travelling up my arms by the runes in my gloves.

I steadied my breath, fighting the rush of power and panic. My magic surged, nearly slipping from my grasp. If I lost control, we were doomed to watch Mikhail win. It all came down to me. I. Would. Not. Fail.

Everything in me cried out to release my magic, and it took my last ounce of strength to hold it back. My arms trembled with the effort. My muscles screamed as though I were lifting three times my body weight.

I forced my eyes open and met Mikhail's gaze.

Whatever happened next, I needed him to know I wasn't one to lose lightly.

The witch's face was slick with blood, as though he'd dipped his head into a pool of it. Red dripped off his nose and slicked back his hair. The whites of his eyes were whiter, his bright teeth brighter.

The madness in his eyes a thousand times more potent.

He believed he'd won.

He believed he'd prepared for every possibility and for everything I might throw at him.

In truth, he had. He'd beaten me. I couldn't say otherwise.

But he should have dealt with me when he had the chance.

Moving quickly enough that I gave him no time to counter my attack, I lurched to my feet and, aiming well away from Barrett and Rhys, released the power I'd built in my hands. Bolts of lightning arced towards the witches nearest me. The screams in the room grew louder, the stench of char assaulted my nose, but my attention was focused on the bolt that struck Mikhail in the chest and threw him onto his back.

More sparks zapped my fingers, and I didn't try to rein them in.

He should have been dead. The wards must have protected him from the brunt of my power, but they wouldn't hold out much longer. His eyes widened as they found mine, and he crawled backwards across the floor until his back hit the wall.

His gaze flitted to the cauldron still hissing its smoke towards the ceiling, and I could almost hear his thoughts.

"You want to know if your incantation has worked enough to protect you from me?" I asked as I stalked towards him. "Spoilers—it hasn't. No demon, no immortality, and now you'll never get to taste it."

My legs trembled, my hands shook. In another moment, I would collapse in an exhausted, worn-out heap. For now, adrenaline kept me going, and I clung to it like a life-preserver.

Mikhail gasped to catch his breath, the sound coming out as an ominous wheeze. I shifted to stand beside him so I could turn to face the room without putting him at my back. Barrett and Rhys rushed towards me as the surviving witches retreated, their expressions stunned, terrified, furious.

"This man tried to kill you tonight." I projected my voice as their leader had done, wanting to make sure every person here understood what was at stake. "You won't want to believe me. You'll want to believe he would have shared his power with you, but when you go home tonight, look at the open wounds where you scratched yourself raw. Look at the stains on your clothes where your blood drained from you for the sake of this monster you followed." I pointed at Mikhail's fallen form, and his followers exchanged a few uncertain glances as some of them backed towards the doors.

"Remember also who you faced tonight," I added. "My name is Katerina Palon, and I suggest you remember it. If anyone attempts to follow in his footsteps—if any one of you comes after me in retaliation for what happened, you'll join the corpses of your unlucky peers."

A few nods, a few wide-eyed stares, and then they cleared out, most at a run, some staggering with weakness. A few couldn't move at all, having lost more blood than the rest, and they slumped to the ground now that the press of bodies wasn't there to keep them up. It would be a busy night for the local emergency rooms, with a lot of unanswered questions, but the survivors should feel damn lucky they were still breathing.

Not to mention grateful.

Rhys reached my side, and I held out my hand. He looped his fingers through mine, and when I squeezed, I was relieved by the strength with which he squeezed back. He might be traumatized—might not sleep for weeks—but he was breathing. Maera wouldn't have cause to kill me.

I let go of Rhys, sank to the floor, and crossed my legs. "All right, Mikhail, are you ready to have a little chat?"

He spat at me and used his feet to push himself backwards, but the wall barred his movements. Barrett sidled up beside him to block any other exit, and I waited patiently for Mikhail to accept his defeat.

"You bitch," he growled. "*That* bitch. She didn't say anything about lightning."

My head swam with relief that I was finally about to get some answers. I leaned forward to rest my elbows on my knees. "Who told you about me, Mikhail? Where did you learn this ritual? Who is this mystery patron of yours?"

He barked out a laugh and pressed his hand to his chest as though the burst of effort hurt. Good.

"Do you really think I'm going to tell you anything? You come in here, you kill my people, you stop me from getting what I've worked for all these years—what I've *earned*—and you think I'm going to hand over information like that?" He shook his head. "She was right about one thing—you're a fool. A naive fool who will always fail because you always think you understand when you have no idea."

Anger tickled the back of my throat, but I quenched it with the memory of what I'd achieved tonight. I'd stopped Mikhail and come out on top. I didn't need to understand much more than that.

"Tell me who—"

He launched himself at me, a spell on his lips. Magic surged towards me, and almost as a reflex, a fireball burst from my hand and flew into his face. The blood dripping down his cheeks caught, his hair caught, and in another moment, his entire body was consumed by red-hot flames.

Barrett and Rhys grabbed my arms and hauled me backwards, putting distance between us before I was consumed by my own fire. The three of us stood and watched him burn.

"Fuck!" I vented as the screams subsided. "I did not mean to do that."

The man had been evil, but he'd taken his knowledge with him. I wanted to know how he'd learned those spells that had nearly taken me down—the sorcery hidden in a witch's spell circle. I needed to know where he'd learned the ritual so I could prevent anyone else from trying to cast it. I needed him alive.

At my side, Barrett shrugged. "Couldn't have happened to a meaner son of a bitch."

I turned to look at him, spotted the raw patch along his neck where he'd nearly scratched through the surface, but I noticed no other similar patches on his hands or face. Rhys bore a few extra marks on his wrists and neck, but not deep enough to have broken through more than the first layer of skin. They'd endured the discomfort and controlled themselves.

They'd trusted me.

Relief and warmth rushed through me, devouring my adrenaline, and in a breath, my legs gave out. Barrett caught me before I hit the floor. He pulled my arm around his neck and tucked his other arm around my waist to bear my weight.

"Tell me again how magic is worth all this shit?" he asked, and the only response I could muster was a rough laugh.

Without another word, Rhys led the way to the door, and we stepped into the night.

We'd come here with a mission, and we'd won. I'd faced part of my past that had haunted my nightmares for years, but even as I set the ritual to bed, the knowledge nagged at me that my past wasn't finished with me yet.

It lurked like a monster in the shadows, waiting to strike, and I had no idea how to prepare for it.

36

Katerina

B ARRETT HELPED ME to the car, and I crawled into the back seat so I could lie down.

"Are you all right?" Rhys asked.

I grunted my response. I would be soon enough. Once my stab wound healed, my blood cooled, and my magic returned. Until then, I was little more than a breathing lump of meat who didn't want to speak to anyone.

But I couldn't afford to be silent. "How about you?"

While Rhys put his thoughts together, Barrett climbed into the driver's seat and pulled into the road. The bumps of the uneven ground did little to help my nausea and growing headache, but I sucked it up.

"That was…" Rhys started, and I braced for him to yell at me for allowing him to get within a hundred kilometres of that fight. What I did not expect when he turned in his seat to face me was for him to exclaim, "You didn't tell me you could shoot *lightning*. What the hell, Kat, that was awesome! I blew up the boat, just like you asked. I waited for the fireworks to start, and those potions are wicked. I thought the whole lake was going to go up in flames the explosion was so big. And I managed to take down two of the witches myself because I swear I Saw them trying to sneak up on me. Like a waking vision or something. It was totally wild. I knew something would happen near that graffiti."

"You also got caught," Barrett pointed out with his usual bland practicality.

Rhys's face flushed, and he sagged against the seat. "Well, yeah. I caught the first two but missed the third that came around the building. But still, I kicked some ass on my first time out."

I chuckled gruffly at his undampened enthusiasm and feared what it meant for our future.

Neither Barrett nor Rhys needed medical attention, and all I needed was rest, so we didn't bother with the hospital or Adrian's house. The only delay was a detour to the drive-thru of an all-night diner so we could stuff ourselves with carbs and fats and oodles of sugar. After we finished, Barrett hit the highway and kept going until we reached my house.

It was still morning, barely ten o'clock. The sky was a warm grey that belied the freezing temperatures, and the darker sky over the freezing water warned of a storm on the way.

But what did that matter? We were home. Safe. Alive.

Although Barrett had turned off the engine, none of us rushed to get out of the car. I didn't know about the others, but for me the awareness that we no longer had anything hanging over our heads left me temporarily immobile.

Barrett moved first. Of course he did. He'd had his ten seconds of discomfort at being caught and almost killed, and now he was ready to move on with his life. He pulled my door open and offered his hand, and I didn't hesitate to take it. Look how much we'd grown in the past few days.

In reality, I was too exhausted to torment him. My strength was sapped, only now starting to return. I needed a hot bath, a cup of tea, and a long, long sleep.

Then we could get back to our regularly scheduled programming of not liking each other.

Rhys, on the other hand, was brimming with golden-retriever energy. The moment he burst out of the car, he bounded through the snow towards the house, nearly slamming into his mother as she rushed outside to greet us.

"Mum! We did it! We burst in on those witches and *bam*! I threw spells at them like *bomp, bomp, bomp,* and they were all 'Ahh!' and kept throwing them back at me, but I was too quick and dodged every single one."

He neglected to mention the part about getting dragged into the middle of a blood-draining ritual, and neither Barrett nor I rushed to fill in the blanks. I doubted anyone would blame us for our cowardice as Maera's expression transitioned from shock to horror to barely restrained fury. We followed Rhys's bubbling energy into the house and through to the kitchen.

"Adrian's asleep?" I asked.

"We crossed paths around six o'clock before he went down," Maera said. "He asked me to pass along his congratulations."

I wished he were awake so I could debrief him the way I used to, but I accepted I'd have to wait in line. Barrett would get to tell him all the good stories first, the bastard.

"Kat was great, mum. *Amazing.* She was throwing fire everywhere, and then Mikhail almost got her, but she went all *zap*! Did you know she could do the lightning thing?" He laughed. "Obviously, Mikhail didn't. The look on his face. Man, that was sick."

It was only when he turned to look at me that I spotted the panic in his eyes and realized his exuberance was a well-placed cover. Yes, there was pride shining through his meadow-greens, but there was also fear and uncertainty, along with a desire for more and a terror of what more might mean.

"Yes, well, that's lovely, Rhys," Maera said, "but perhaps we can leave the battle talk until after I've had some tea, all right?"

She shook her head and went straight for the kettle. I suspected if it had been a few hours later, there would have been some brandy slipped in amongst the tea leaves.

Maybe there would be anyway.

Beneath her nonchalant response was a trembling vein of emotion. I didn't blame her. Yes, Rhys had held up incredibly well for his first time out, but she was no fool. The three of us were covered in secondhand blood, exhausted, and dazed. Although we'd all come out in one piece, she had to know it had been closer than her son was letting on.

Later, I was sure, there would be a heavy conversation between us, but for now, she leaned her hip against the counter and didn't take her eyes off Rhys as the water boiled. When she caught me watching her, she tipped her chin in acknowledgement, and I nodded back. I'd kept my promise as best I could. It hadn't been foolproof, and I'd nearly failed, but when it mattered, I'd found my strength and protected my family.

I was as grateful to Rhys for reminding me of who I wanted to be as Maera was to me for keeping him safe.

Barrett slapped the younger man on the back. "You did well, Byrne. We couldn't have asked for a better third. You followed orders, did your best to stay out of trouble, and proved you have great aim. That's the best you can hope for most days. When you're up for it, we'll continue your training, get you comfortable with a blade or two in your hands."

"Maybe some shooting lessons, too?" Rhys asked. "Knives are great and all, but they have to get too close for me to use them. Something with distance would probably be best, wouldn't it?"

Barrett nodded. "We can look at getting you a firearms licence, though I'll warn you guns don't always work well in a fight against magicals. Their spells can muck about with the mechanisms. Useful to have, but not good to rely on. Knives are a safer bet."

"Unless you have potions." I wouldn't begrudge Barrett sharing his knowledge, but Rhys lived under my roof. It wouldn't do to let the soldier turn him against all things magical.

Rhys blushed and handed over the empty satchel he'd reclaimed on our way to the car. "I used almost all the ones you gave me. Probably could have held a few back, but—"

I shook my head. "You did what you had to do. Once I track down Poppy, we'll see that you're fully stocked."

I snuck a peek at Maera to see how she was handling this little discussion, and to my lack of surprise, she'd turned her back on us. Her shoulders were tense, and her hand was pressed to her face. I was certain that if she turned around, her cheeks would be wet with tears.

Swallowing my guilt, I crossed the kitchen and poured the hot water into the teapot.

"I hate this," Maera said to me, her voice low enough that I doubted she meant for Rhys to hear. "Guns? Knives? I didn't raise my son to be a fighter."

I put my arm around her, and she sagged against me. "It's not my first choice, either. Anything I can do to keep him out of danger, I will. But he needs to learn how to defend himself."

She gave a resigned nod.

"I'm in this now, mum," Rhys said from the table. Gone was the bright wildness in his eyes that had been there since we'd arrived home. In its place was a seriousness I'd only seen from him a handful of times in his eighteen years. "For the past four years, I've wondered why I was cursed with visions that sucked out so much of my life and left me more confused than anything. I haven't been able to get past them. With Kat and Barrett, I felt like I'd finally figured out what I'm supposed to do. Seeing those witches try to gain more power, preventing Mikhail from killing them all—*that* is why I was born a Seer. I can't turn my back on that world now that I've seen how I can help."

"I know," she said, sounding so much older than her fifty-five years. "I don't need to like it, but I accept it." Her back straightened, and her next words came out lined with steel. "But if you're stepping your foot deeper into that world, so am I."

"Maera—" I started, and she turned to meet my eye.

"I don't mean joining you in the fight, Katerina, but I won't be kept in the dark. I also won't sit back and let you drag my son into danger if you keep showing the same half-hearted energy I've seen in you since I was a child. I know you can do better. If Rhys is taking this step with you, I'll be there to make sure you stay at your best. I will be on your back to keep you focused. Is that understood?"

The fire in her eyes ignited a matching flame in my soul, and I nodded, not with reluctance, not with resentment, but with gratitude. I had a fresh outlook on life, a new drive to carry on breathing, and I appreciated anything that helped me hang on to it.

I couldn't afford to slide back into the dreary apathy I'd lost myself in with the shifting times. Not if I wanted to keep my sanity. Or my humanity.

If Maera wanted to take on that headache, I would submit to it with pleasure. Especially if it meant increasing the odds that Rhys would be safe at my side.

As Barrett, Rhys, and Maera sat around the table, I pulled myself onto the kitchen counter. Maera poured four cups of tea, then went to the pantry and pulled out a basket of fresh-baked biscuits. She set them on the table, and the three of them tucked into an impromptu snack of comfort and companionship. I watched from my perch and tried to identify the sudden tingling in my chest—the warm vibration of something I hadn't felt in far too long.

When I finally put a name to it, my throat closed, and I allowed myself a smile as I slid off the counter and joined the others at the table.

It was the feeling of connection.

It was the feeling of coming home.

Epilogue

Katerina

BY THE TIME Adrian woke up that night, I was mostly recovered. Physically, anyway. Magically, I felt as though I'd pulled a muscle by wrangling lightning the way I had, and mentally and emotionally, my status was questionable, which my friend recognized immediately.

He bundled me into a tight hug and pressed a kiss against my hair. "Whatever happened, Katerina, you prevented so much worse."

He'd repeated those same words to me hundreds of times over the past eight centuries. Whenever I'd felt guilty about a kill or believed I hadn't done enough.

Always, he was my voice of perspective, and I was glad he was here.

"Thanks for leaving your house for me," I mumbled into his neck.

He chuckled. "You can always be sure of that much, tesoro. I would never deprive myself of your company. Please don't stay away so long next time."

"I won't."

"And I'll be sure to pass along your thanks to Emrick for suggesting I come visit you."

I stiffened and pulled away from him, my smile fragile. "Please do. It was kind of him to think of it."

His eyebrow quirked. "Kind, indeed."

I levelled a stare at him, and he shrugged, wisely choosing not to push the issue.

As soon as they could, Barrett and Adrian left for home, and not long later, Rhys and Maera headed to bed.

Alone in the silence, I retreated to my private balcony and dropped into one of my Muskoka chairs. I pulled my knees to my chest with my oversized T-shirt tugged overtop of them, wrapped my arms around my legs, and stared out at the blue-and-white vista of moonlight on snow.

With nothing else to occupy my mind—except for the one person I always struggled not to think about—memories of the fight with Mikhail flurried past me. The expressions on the witches' faces as I released the full strength of my fire magic. The shouts of surprise as the lightning burst from my palms. Mikhail's sneer when I'd asked how he'd learned about the ritual.

I thought of the way the fire had devoured him, taking his answers with him.

It nagged at me, who his mysterious patron was. I had no doubt Adrian would continue to dig into it. Once I recovered, I would turn my attention to the remaining Death Raisers to find out if someone had been foolish enough to return to the coven after the last time I'd decimated them.

With luck, I'd soon know who I was dealing with. Then I could hunt them down and burn that cursed spell.

Already on a roll towards the past, my thoughts continued further back. My mother's smile came to mind, and the way she would put her arms around me whenever I made her proud. Would she have been impressed by the way I'd dealt with Mikhail, or would she have been disappointed that I hadn't found a way to stop him without killing him?

Almost nine hundred years, and the habit of asking the universe what my parents would think hadn't faded. Nor did the ache in my heart at the knowledge that I would never know.

I liked to think that, like me, she would sit somewhere in the middle—regretful that it had ended the way it had but accepting the necessity. My father would have given me a solemn nod, appreciating that I'd made the only decision I could. Kyla would have rolled her eyes and asked why I'd bothered trying to talk to him at all. But she'd only been sixteen when she died, so the impetuousness of youth would have been with her still.

And Gran, well, Gran would have understood better than any of them. Not only my actions, but everything I'd felt during each moment. She would never have let me reach such a point of indifference in my life, but her response wouldn't have been one of disappointment or reproach. Only sadness that I'd lost my way.

You are enough, nephene, she would have said to me, and from her lips, maybe I would have believed it.

Maybe.

The moonlight shifted from behind the clouds and spilled across the balcony to cover my arms. I reached my hand towards it, allowed its light to caress my skin. As it did, I closed my eyes and imagined the touch becoming tangible. I felt the warmth of long, callused fingers running up my arms, soft lips brushing against my neck, a broad chest pressing against my side. I sank into every sensation, travelling the wave of comfort, security, and desire.

There had been a time when, after such a fight, after such a day of revelations, I would have wanted nothing more than to relax in Death's embrace for a few hours or days, seeking comfort in Emrick's deep voice and soft-spoken words. I would have savoured his reassurances that I had done the right thing, and his praise that I had surpassed my own expectations. There was no one who made my blood sing the way he did, who made the earth spin and the moon rise and set.

But if my memories and my long years had taught me anything, it was that all things came to an end, and even love could be tainted by the harsh realities of the world. A whole life could be shattered and change course because of the loss of a single person's presence.

Even as I told myself these things, I opened my eyes and turned to the space beside me. I didn't know if I was more relieved or disappointed to find it empty.

Emrick

Moonlight fell across the snow, highlighting the ridges and grooves of the ice sculptures peppered across Adrian's property.

I stood on the edge of the balcony, staring over it, feeling as distant and empty as the blank-eyed stares of the dragons, wolves, and lovers guarding the paths. A sharp wind blew around me, tugging at my hair and my sweater, but I didn't feel the cold. I barely remembered what cold was. It had been too long.

Heat, though. That was as real and familiar to me as the rising and setting of the sun. The burn of Katerina's kiss, the warmth of her body as it pressed against mine.

After seventy-five years, I'd thought those memories had begun to fade, but being in her presence again this week had brought them back with such force, I still hadn't caught my breath.

The Fates were cruel, and there was nothing I could do about it except hope for a change.

"Emrick," Adrian said behind me as he stepped onto the balcony. "I'm glad you're here."

I didn't turn around as my old friend joined me. My mouth was dry, and my heart pattered an uncomfortable rhythm in my chest. "How is she doing?"

I didn't have to explain myself. Not to Adrian. Thank the gods, because I knew how pitiful I'd sound if I tried.

He leaned his forearms on the railing and stared out over his winter garden. "She'll survive, of course. She always does." His expression shifted with his faint smile. "It's too bad she had to kill him, really."

I agreed. I would have enjoyed doing the honours myself.

"I would have liked the opportunity to thank him," Adrian continued.

My eyebrows climbed. "Oh?"

He chuckled. "The next time you see her, you'll understand."

I huffed and settled on the railing beside him. "Whenever that might be."

"I suspect it will be sooner than you think."

I turned to face him. He was holding something back from me. Not unusual. Adrian enjoyed wrapping himself in an air of mystery. He felt it added to his charms, no matter how often Kat and I had argued to the contrary.

No hint of a smile touched his features now, however. His brown eyes were dark, the set of his shoulders stiff.

"Have you felt it, Emrick? The feeling of change in the air?"

I released a slow breath. "I have. Rumbles in the afterlife. Rumours of trouble in the magical world. More than one soul has crossed by their own hand, talking about the writing on the wall."

Whatever this supposed trouble was, it had created vibrations in the air that had chased me through this world, the afterlife, and in between. A growing shadow with a million eyes that always knew where to find me, though so far I hadn't been able to discover what it was after.

"Do you ever get the sense that your time is dwindling?" Adrian asked.

The seeming change of subject took me by surprise. A bitter laugh bubbled deep in my gut, and I let it spill out. "No, I can't say I do. My life stretches along an endless, grey road. Believing otherwise, even for a moment, would be a welcome relief." I frowned and looked more closely at my old friend. "You?"

Adrian nodded, his young, handsome face tight as he stared out over the snow. "For the first time in two thousand years, I have this feeling of sand running through my fingers. It doesn't frighten me, but I do worry for those around me." He pushed away from the railing and met my questioning stare. "If something happens to me, if I don't survive whatever this change is, do you promise to watch out for Katerina?"

I stiffened. "You're asking me to go against the promise I made to stay away from her?"

The sparkle returned to Adrian's eyes, as though he knew as well as I did that I was doomed to break that promise a million times. "I am," he said. "I can't help but think she's going to need you."

"You know I would never let anything happen to her."

Adrian nodded, relieved, and silence fell over us as we turned to stare into the night, both of us lost in our thoughts. Adrian's expression suggested his were calm, at peace with whatever was coming.

I didn't feel nearly as steady. I'd always known my path would cross with Kat's again at some point. I'd just hoped it would be under happier circumstances.

But my years on this earth had taught me that getting what you wanted always came at a cost.

Whatever fires of hell I needed to walk through, I would willingly take those first steps.

The change that was coming would have to be ready to face us both.

Thank You for Reading

Thank you so much for taking a chance on an independent author. We're living in a wonderful age where it's easy to upload a book to the internet, but that doesn't reflect the blood, sweat, and tears that go into making a book the best version it can be. It takes time, patience, perseverance, and to have the final result end up in a new reader's hands is the best reward. You are the reason we keep writing, so thank you.

If you enjoyed the read, please help support the author by leaving a review at the retailer where you purchased the book. Reviews make a world of difference for an author, helping us reach new audiences and bringing more people into the worlds you've spent time in.

For exclusive character content, announcements, promotions, and special offers, sign up for Krista's mailing list at https://www.kristawalshauthor.com/pages/about-the-author

Acknowledgements

I reached a point back in 2016 or so where I believed Kat & Emrick's story would never be told. I saw the rest of the story in broad strokes, but not clearly enough to write it.

Until I realized the ultimate truth: first and foremost, this is a love story.

Not only between Kat and Emrick, but between Kat and her chosen family. And as soon as I realized that, the rest came to me like a fireball in the face.

Now they're here—they're really, really here—and I have a few people to thank for making it happen:

Kate Sparkes, my beautiful, wonderful, amazing friend. You keep me honest and never let me get away with cutting corners on character development. Please stay with me forever.

The FAKAs, my incredible writers' group, who've helped me level up in so many ways, I'm ready to take on some boss fights.

Christopher Barnes, editor, cheerleader. Thank you for cleaning up my prose, even if you loathe all my colons.

My ARC readers and Street Team—with you behind me, how can Kat & Emrick's story not be read by so many people who might not have found them otherwise? Any wide success of this book? All at your door.

My Patrons… just wow. From my the bottom of my heart, your support means everything to me.

Traci, Mardie, Becca—thank you for your beta reading eyes (and extra thanks to Amy, Becca, and Kimmy for helping me come up with the names of the new age shops throughout this series)

Chris Reddie, monster builder, father extraordinaire. Thank you for wrangling our beautiful, adventurous, energetic child and giving me a chance to work on my neverending deadlines. I promise it'll slow down soon. Promise.

And always last but never, ever least, my readers. The more I get to know many of you across the emails and socials and markets, the more I'm grateful to have you in my life. Your words of support and encouragement never go unnoticed. The next book is always because of you.

About the Author

Known for witty, vivid characters, Krista Walsh never has more fun than getting them into trouble and taking her time getting them out.

When not writing, she can be found reading, gaming, or watching a film – anything to get lost in a good story.

She currently lives in Ottawa, Ontario with her husband, toddler, and epileptic blue heeler.

You can find her at www.kristawalshauthor.com or at the local Second Cup coffee shop... but only if you come bearing a Vanilla Bean Latte, half-sweet.

Other Works by Krista Walsh

Epic Fantasy

The Meratis Trilogy
The Cadis Trilogy
The Nayis Trilogy

Urban Fantasy

The Dark Descendants
The Ghostmaker Trilogy
The Immortal Sorceress Series